The darkness made the portraits difficult to see, but he thought he recognized the light and shadow work of a Daguerre portrait and yet—and yet—something differed, distorted, perhaps, by the dream.

"They will make you great," said a voice behind him.

He turned, and saw a woman. At least, he thought it was a woman. Her hair was cropped above her ears, and she wore trousers.

"Who will make me great?" he asked.

"The pictures," she said. "People will remember them for generations."

He took a step closer to her, but she smiled and touched his palm. The shadows turned black and the dream faded into a gently, restful sleep.

ALSO BY
KRISTINE KATHRYN RUSCH

THE DIVING SERIES

Diving into the Wreck: A Diving Novel

City of Ruins: A Diving Novel

Becalmed: A Diving Universe Novella

The Application of Hope: A Diving Universe Novella

Boneyards: A Diving Novel

Skirmishes: A Diving Novel

The Runabout: A Diving Novel

The Falls: A Diving Universe Novel

Searching for the Fleet: A Diving Novel

The Spires of Denon: A Diving Universe Novella

The Renegat: A Diving Universe Novel

Escaping Amnthra: A Diving Universe Novella

The Court-Martial of the Renegat Renegades

Thieves: A Diving Novel

Squishy's Teams: A Diving Universe Novel

The Chase: A Diving Novel

Maelstrom: A Diving Universe Novella

THE FEY SERIES

Writing as Kris Nelscott

THE SMOKEY DALTON SERIES

A Dangerous Road

Smoke-Filled Rooms

Thin Walls

Stone Cribs

War at Home

Days of Rage

Street Justice

AND

Protectors

———

Writing as Kristine Grayson

The Charming Trilogy, Vol. 1

The Charming Trilogy, Vol. 2

The Fates Trilogy

The Daughters of Zeus Trilogy

THE GALLERY OF HIS DREAMS

KRISTINE KATHRYN RUSCH

WMG
PUBLISHING

The Gallery of His Dreams
Copyright © 2024 by Kristine Kathryn Rusch
First published in 1991 by Axolotl Press, a subsidiary of Pulphouse
Publishing, and *Asimov's Science Fiction Magazine*
Published by WMG Publishing
Cover and layout copyright © 2024 by WMG Publishing
Cover design by WMG Publishing
Cover art copyright © lauraliu | Depositphotos, Mathew B. Brady (Six
Pounder Wiard Gun, Wash., Arsenal, 1862)/Library of Congress

ISBN-13 (trade paperback): 978-1-56146-992-5
ISBN-13 (hardcover): 978-1-56146-898-0

For Dean

THE GALLERY OF HIS DREAMS

Let him who wishes to know what war is look at this series of illustrations.... It was so nearly like visiting the battlefield to look over these views, that all the emotions excited by the actual sight of the stained and sordid scene, strewed with rags and wrecks, came back to us, and we buried them in the recesses of our cabinet as we would have buried the mutilated remains of the dead they too vividly represented.

~ OLIVER WENDELL HOLMES

1838

Brady leaned against a hay bale and felt the blades dig into his back. He smelled of pig dung and his own sweat, and his muscles ached. His da had gone to the pump to wash up, and then into the cowshed, but Brady claimed he needed a rest. His da, never one to argue with relaxation, let him sit against the hay bales. Brady didn't dare stay too long; if his ma saw him, she would be on the front porch, yelling insults unintelligible through her Irish brogue.

He did need to think, though. Milking cows and cleaning the pig pen didn't give him enough time to make plans. He couldn't stay on the farm the rest of his life, he knew that. He hated the work, the animals, the smell, and the long hours that all led to a poor, subsistence living. His da thought the farm a step up from the hovel he had grown up in and certainly an improvement from Brady's grandfather's life back in the Old Country. Brady often wished he could see what his da's or his grandfather's life had really been like. But he had to trust their memories, memories that, at least in his grandfather's case, had become more and more confusing as the years progressed.

Brady pulled a strand of hay from the bale, sending a burst of sharp fresh summer-scent around him. He wanted more than a ruined farm and a few livestock in upstate New York. Mr. Hanley, his teacher, had pulled Brady aside on the day he left school, and reminded him that in the United States of American even farmboys could become great men. Mr. Hanley used to start the school day by telling the boys that the late President Thomas Jefferson defined the nation's creed when he wrote that all men were created equal, and President Andrew Jackson had proven the statement true with his election not ten years before.

Brady didn't want to be president. He wanted to do something different, something he couldn't even imagine now. He wanted to be great—and he wanted to be remembered.

1840

The spring thaw had turned the streets of New York City into rivers.

Brady laughed as he jumped from one sidewalk board to the next, then turned and waited for Page to jump. Page hesitated a moment, running a slender hand through his beard. Then he jumped and landed, one tattered shoe in the cold water, one out. Brady grabbed his friend's arm and pulled him up.

"Good Lord, William, how far away is this man's home?"

"He's not just any man," Page said, shaking the water off his legs. "He's a painter, and a damn fine one."

Brady smiled. Page was a painter himself and had, a few months earlier, opened a studio below their joint apartment. Brady helped with the rent on the studio as a repayment for Page's help in moving Brady from the farm. Being a clerk at A.T. Stewart's largest store was an improvement over farm life—the same kind of improvement that Brady's father had made. Only Brady wasn't going to stop there. Page had promised to help by showing Brady how to paint. While Brady had an eye for composition, he lacked the firm hand, the easy grace of a portraitist. Page had been polite; he hadn't said that Brady was hopeless. But they both knew that Mathew B. Brady would never make his living with a paintbrush in his hand.

Brady braced himself against a wooden building as he stepped over a submerged portion of sidewalk. "You haven't said what this surprise is."

"I don't know what the surprise is. Samuel simply said that he had learned about it in France and that we would be astonished." Page slipped into a thin alley between buildings and then pulled open a door. Brady followed, and found himself staring up a dark flight of stairs. Page was already halfway up, his wet shoe squeaking with each step. Brady gripped the railing and took the stairs two at a time.

Page opened the door, sending light across the stairs. Brady reached the landing just as Page bellowed, "Samuel!" Brady peered inside, nearly choking on the scent of linseed and turpentine.

Large windows graced the walls, casting dusty sunlight on a room filled with canvases. Dropcloths covered most of the canvases and some of the furniture scattered about. A desk, overflowing with papers, stood under one window. Near that a large wooden box dwarfed a rickety table. A stoop-shouldered long-haired man braced the table with one booted foot.

"Over here, Page, over here. Don't dawdle. Help me move this thing. The damn table is about to collapse."

Page scurried across the room, bent down, and grabbed an edge of the box. The man picked up the other side and led the way to his desk. He balanced the box with one hand and his knee while his other hand swept the desk clean. They set the box down and immediately the man pulled out a handkerchief and wiped away the sweat that had dripped into his bushy eyebrows.

"I meant to show you in a less dramatic fashion," he said, then looked up. Brady whipped his hat off his head and held it with both hands. The man had sharp eyes, eyes that could see right through a person, clear down to his dreams.

"Well?" the man said.

Brady nodded. He wouldn't be stared down. "I'm Mathew B. Brady, sir."

"Samuel F. B. Morse." Morse tucked his handkerchief back into his pocket and clasped his hands behind his back. "You must be the boy Page has been telling me about. He assumes you have some sort of latent talent."

Brady glanced at Page. Page blushed, the color seeping through the patches of skin still visible through his beard.

"Hmmm," Morse said as he stalked forward. He paced around Brady, studied him for a moment. "You're what, eighteen?"

"Almost, sir."

"If you had talent, you'd know it by now." Morse shook his head. His suit smelled faintly of mothballs. "No, no. You're one of the lucky ones, blessed with drive. A man with talent merely has a head start. A man with drive succeeds."

Morse stalked back to his desk, stepping on the papers that littered the floor. "Drive but no talent. I have the perfect machine for you." He put his hand on the box. "Ever hear of Louis Daguerre? No, of course not. What would a farmboy know of the latest scientific discoveries?"

Brady started, then shot another look at Page. Perhaps Page had said something about Brady's background. Page ignored him and had come closer to Morse.

"Daguerre found a way to preserve the world in one image. Look." He handed Page a small metal plate. As Page tilted it toward the light, Brady saw the Unitarian Church he walked past almost every day.

"This is a daguerreotype," Morse said. "I made this one through the window of the third floor staircase at New York University."

"That is the right view," Page's voice held awe. "You used no paints."

"I used this," Morse said, his hand pounding on the

box's top. "It has a lens here—" and he pointed at the back end from which a glass-topped cylinder protruded "—and a place here for the plates. The plates are silver on copper, which I treat with iodine and expose to light through the lens. Then I put the plate in another box containing heated mercury, and when I'm done—an image! An exact reproduction of the world in black and white."

Brady touched the cool edge of the plate. "It preserves memories," he said, thinking that if such a device had existed before, he could have seen his father's hovel, his grandfather's home.

"It does more than that, son," Morse said. "This is our future. It will destroy portrait painting. Soon everything will be images on metal, keepsakes for generations to come."

Page pulled back at the remark about portrait painting. He went to the window, looked at the street below. "I suppose that's why you brought us up here. To show me that I'll be out of work soon?"

"No, lad." Morse laughed and the sound boomed and echoed off the canvas-covered walls. "I want to save you, not destroy you. I'm opening a school to teach this new process and I invite you to join. Fifty dollars tuition for the entire semester and I promise you'll be a better portraitist when you're done than you are now."

Page gave Morse a sideways look. Page's back was rigid and his hands were clenched in trembling fists. Brady could almost feel his friend's rage. "I paint." Page spoke with a slow deliberation. "I have no need for what will clearly become a poor man's art."

Morse did not seem offended by Page's remark. "And you, young Brady. Will you use your drive to acquire a talent?"

Brady stared at the plate and mysterious box. Fifty dollars was a lot of money, but he already had twenty set aside for a trip home. Page did say he had an eye for composition. And if a man with an eye for composition, a lot of drive, and a little talent took Daguerre's Box all over the world, he would be able to send his memories back to the people left behind.

Brady smiled. "Yes," he said. "I'll take your class."

He would postpone the trip to see his parents, and raise the rest of the money somehow. Page whirled away from the window as if Brady had betrayed him. But Brady didn't care. When they got home, he would explain it all. And it was so simple. He had another improvement to make.

1840

That night, Brady dreamed. He stood in a large cool room, darkened and hidden in shadows. He bumped into a wall and found himself touching a ribbed column—a Doric column, he believed. He took cautious steps forward, stumbled, then caught himself on a piece of painted wood. His hands slid up the rough edges until he realized he was standing beside a single-horse carriage. He felt his way around to the back. The carriage box had no windows, but the back stood wide open. He climbed inside. The faint rotten-egg smell of sulphur rose. He bumped against a box and glass rattled. A wagon filled with equipment. He climbed out, feeling like he was snooping. There was more light now. He saw a wall ahead of him, covered with portraits.

The darkness made the portraits difficult to see, but he

thought he recognized the light and shadow work of a Daguerre portrait and yet—and yet—something differed, distorted, perhaps, by the dream. And he knew he was in a dream. The cool air was too dry, the walls made of a foreign substance, the lights (what he could see of them), glass-encased boxes on the ceiling. The portraits were of ghastly things: dead men and stark fields, row after row of demolished buildings. On several, someone had lettered his last name in flowing white script.

"They will make you great," said a voice behind him. He turned, and saw a woman. At least, he thought it was a woman. Her hair was cropped above her ears, and she wore trousers.

"Who will make me great?" he asked.

"The pictures," she said. "People will remember them for generations." He took a step closer to her, but she smiled and touched his palm. The shadows turned black and the dream faded into a gently, restful sleep.

1849

Brady leaned against the hand-carved wooden railing. The candles on the large chandelier burned steady, while the candelabras flickered in the breezes left by the dancing couples. A pianist, a violinist, and a cello player—all, Mr. Handy had assured him, very well respected—played the newest European dance, the waltz, from one corner of the huge ballroom. Mothers cornered their daughters along the wall, approving dance cards, and shaking fans at impertinent young males. The staircase opened into the ballroom, and Brady didn't want to cross the threshold. He had never been to a dance like this before. His only experiences dancing had been at gatherings Page had taken him to when he first arrived in New York. He knew none of the girls, except Samuel Handy's daughter Juliette, and she was far too pretty for Brady to approach.

So he watched her glide across the floor with young man after young man, her hooped skirts swaying, her brown hair in ringlets, her eyes sparkling, and her cheeks flushed. Handy had told him that at the age of four, she had been presented to President Jackson. She had been so beautiful, Handy said, that Jackson had wanted to adopt her. Brady was glad he hadn't seen her as a child, glad he had seen the mature beauty. When he finished taking the portraits of her father, he would ask if he could take one of her. The wet-plate process would let him make copies, and he would keep one in his own rooms, just so that he could show his friends how very lovely she was.

The waltz ended, and Juliet curtsied to her partner, then left the floor. Her dance card swung from her wrist and the diamonds around her neck caught the candlelight. Too late, Brady realized she was coming to see him.

"I have one spot left on my dance card," she said as she stopped in front of him. She smelled faintly of lilacs, and he knew he would have to keep a sprig near her portrait every spring. "And I was waiting for you to fill it."

Brady blushed. "I barely know you, Miss Juliet."

She batted his wrist lightly with her fan. "Julia," she said. "And I know you better than half the boys here. You have spent three days in my daddy's house, Mr. Brady, and your conversation at dinner has been most entertaining. I was afraid that I bored you."

"No, no," he said. The words sounded so formal. How could he joke with his female clients and let this slip of a girl intimidate him? "I would love to take that slot on your dance card, Miss Juliet."

"Julia," she said again. "I hate being named after a stupid little minx who died for nothing. I think when a woman loves, it is her duty to love intelligently, don't you?"

"Yes," Brady said, although he had no idea what she was talking about. "And I'm Mathew."

"Wonderful, Mathew." Her smile added a single dimple to her left cheek. She extended her card to him and he penciled his name in for the next dance, filling the bottom of the first page. The music started—another waltz—and she took his hand. He followed her onto the floor, placed one hand on her cinched waist, and held the other lightly in his own. They circled around the floor, the tip of her skirt brushing against his pants leg. She didn't smile at him. Instead her eyes were very serious and her lips were pursed and full.

"You don't do this very often, do you, Mathew?"

"No," he said. In fact, he felt as if he were part of a dream—the musicians, the beautifully garbed women, the house servants blending into the wallpaper. Everything at the Handy plantation had an air of almost too much sensual pleasure. "I work, probably too much."

"I have seen what you do, Mathew, and I think it is a wondrous magic." A slight flush crept into her cheeks, whether from the exertion or her words, Brady couldn't tell. She lowered her voice. "I dreamed about you last night. I dreamed I was in a beautiful large gallery with light clearer than sunlight, and hundreds of people milled about, looking at your portraits on the wall. They all talked about you, how marvelous your work was, and how it influenced them. You're a great man, Mathew, and I am flattered at the interest you have shown in me."

The music stopped and she slipped from his arms, stopping to chat with another guest as she wandered toward the punch table. Brady stood completely still, his heart pounding against his chest. She had been to the gallery of his dreams. She knew about his future. The musicians began another piece, and Brady realized how foolish he must look, standing in the center of the dance floor. He dodged whirling couples and made his way to the punch table, hoping that he could be persuasive enough to convince Julia Handy to let him replace all those other names on the remaining half of her dance card.

1861

He woke up with the idea, his body sweat-covered and shimmering with nervous energy. If he brought a wagon with him, it would work: a wagon like the one he had dreamed about the night he had met Morse.

Brady moved away from his sleeping wife and stepped onto the bare hardwood. The floor creaked. He glanced at Julia, but she didn't awaken. The bedroom was hot; Washington in July had a muggy air. If the rumors were to be believed, the first battle would occur in a matter of days. He had so little time. He had thought he would never come up with a way to record the war.

He had started recording history with his book, THE GALLERY OF ILLUSTRIOUS AMERICANS. He had hoped to continue by taking portraits of the impending war, but he hadn't been able to figure out how. The wet plates had to be developed right after the portrait had been taken. He needed a way to take the equipment with him. The answer was so simple, he was amazed he had to dream it.

But that dream had haunted him for years now. And when he had learned the wet-plate process, discovered that the rotten-egg smell of sulphur was part of it, the dream had come back to him as vividly as an old memory. That had been years ago. Now, with the coming war, he found himself thinking of the portraits of demolished buildings, and the woman's voice, telling him he would be great.

He would have to set up a special war fund. The president had given him a pass to make portraits of the army on the field, but had stressed that Brady would have to use his own funds. As Lincoln told Brady with only a hint of humor, the country was taking enough gambles already.

Small price, Brady figured, to record history. He was, after all, a wealthy man.

1861

Julia had hoped to join the picnickers who sat on the hills overlooking the battlefield, but Brady was glad he had talked her out of it. He pulled the wet plate out of his camera and placed the plate into the box. The portrait would be of smoke and tiny men clashing below him. He glanced at the farmhouse, and the army that surrounded it. They seemed uneasy, as if this battle wasn't what they expected. It wasn't what he had expected, either. The confusion, the smoke, even the heat made sense. The screaming did not.

Brady put the plate in its box, then set the box in his wagon. Before the day was out, he would return to Washington, set the plates, and send portraits to the illustrated magazines. The wagon was working out better than he expected. The illustrations would probably earn him yet another award.

The cries seemed to grow louder, and above them, he heard a faint rumbling. He checked the sky for clouds and saw nothing. The smoke gave the air an acrid tinge and made the heat seem even hotter. A bead of sweat ran down the side of his face. He grabbed the camera and lugged it back to the wagon, then returned for the tripod. He was proud of himself; he had expected to be afraid and yet his hands were as steady as they had been inside his studio.

He closed up the back of the wagon, waved his assistant, Tim O'Sullivan, onto the wagon, and climbed aboard. O'Sullivan sat beside him and clucked the horse onto Bull Run road. The army's advance had left ruts so deep that the wagon tilted at an odd angle. The rumble was growing louder. Overhead, something whistled and then a cannonball landed off to one side, spraying dirt and muck over the two men. The horse shrieked and reared; Brady felt the reins cut through his fingers. The wagon rocked, nearly tipped, then righted itself. Brady turned, and saw a dust cloud rising behind him. A mass of people was running toward him.

"Lord a mercy," he whispered, and thrust the reins at O'Sullivan. O'Sullivan looked at them as if he had never driven the wagon before. "I'm going to get the equipment. Be ready to move on my signal."

O'Sullivan brought the horse to a stop and Brady leapt

off the side. He ran to the back, opened the door, grabbed his camera, and set up just in time to take portraits of soldiers running past. Both sides—Union and Confederate—wore blue, and Brady couldn't tell which troops were scurrying past him. He could smell the fear, the human sweat, see the strain in the men's eyes. His heart had moved to his throat, and he had to concentrate to shove a wet plate into the camera. He uncapped the lens, hoping that the scene wouldn't change too much, that in his precious three seconds, he would capture more than a blur.

Mixed with the soldiers were women, children, and well-dressed men—some still clutching picnic baskets, others barely holding their hats. All ran by. A few loose horses galloped near Brady; he had to hold the tripod steady. He took portrait after portrait, seeing faces he recognized—like that silly newspaper correspondent Russell, the man who had spread the word about Brady's poor eyesight—mouths agape, eyes wide in panic. As Brady worked, the sounds blended into each other. He couldn't tell the human screams from the animal shrieks and the whistle of mortar. Bullets whizzed past, and more than one lodged in the wagon. The wagon kept lurching, and Brady knew that O'Sullivan was having trouble holding the horse.

Suddenly the wagon rattled away from him. Brady turned, knocked over the tripod himself, and watched in horror as people trampled his precious equipment. He started to get down, to save the camera, then realized that in their panic, the people would run over him. He grabbed what plated he could, shoved them into the pocket of his great coat, and joined the throng, running after the wagon, shouting at O'Sullivan to stop.

But the wagon didn't stop. It kept going around the winding, twisting corners of the road, until it disappeared in the dust cloud. Another cannonball landed beside the road and Brady cringed as dirt spattered him. A woman screamed and fell forward, blood blossoming on her back. He turned to help her, but the crowd pushed him forward. He couldn't stop even if he wanted to.

This was not romantic; it was not the least bit pretty. It had cost him hundreds of dollars in equipment and might cost him his life if he didn't escape soon. This was what the history books had never told him about war, had never explained about the absolute mess, the dirt and the blood. Behind him, he heard screaming, someone shouting that the black cavalry approached, the dreaded black cavalry of the Confederacy, worse than the four horses of the apocalypse, if the illustrated newspapers were to be believed, and Brady ran all the harder. His feet slipped in the ruts in the road and he nearly tripped, but he saw other people down, other people trampled, and he knew he couldn't fall.

He rounded a corner, and there it was, the wagon, on its side, the boxes spilling out, the plates littering the dirt road. O'Sullivan was on his hands and knees, trying to clean up, his body shielded only because the carriage wall made the fleeing people reroute.

Brady hurried over the carriage side, ignoring the split wood, the bullet holes, and the fact that the horse was missing. Tears were running down the side of O'Sullivan's face, but the man seemed oblivious to them. Brady grabbed O'Sullivan's arm, and pulled him up. "Come on, Tim," he said. "Black cavalry on the hills. We've got to get away."

"The plates—" O'Sullivan said.

"Forget the plates. We've got to get out of here."

"The horse spooked and broke free. I think someone stole her, Mat."

O'Sullivan was shouting, but Brady could barely hear him. His lungs were choked and he thought he was going to drown in dust. "We have to go," he said.

He yanked O'Sullivan forward, and they rejoined the crowd. They ran until Brady could run no longer; his lungs burned and his side ached. Bullets continued to penetrate, and Brady saw too many men in uniform motionless on the side of the road.

"The crowd itself is a target," he said, not realizing he had spoken aloud. He tightened his grip on O'Sullivan's arm and led him off the road into the thin trees. They trudged straight ahead, Brady keeping the setting sun to his left, and soon the noises of battle disappeared behind them. They stopped and Brady leaned against a thick oak to catch his breath. The sun had gone down and it was getting cool.

"What now?" O'Sullivan asked.

"If we don't meet any rebs, we're safe," Brady said. He took off his hat, wiped the sweat off his brow with his sleeve, and put his hat back on. Julia would have been very angry with him if he had lost that hat.

"But how do we get back?" O'Sullivan asked.

An image of the smashed equipment rose in Brady's mind along with the broken, overturned horseless wagon. "We walk, Tim." Brady sighed. "We walk."

1861

J ulia watched as he stocked up the new wagon. She said nothing as he lugged equipment inside, new equipment he had purchased from Anthony's supply house on extended credit. He didn't want to hurt his own business by taking away needed revenue, and the Anthonys were willing to help—especially after they had seen the quality of his war work for the illustrated newspapers.

"I can't come with you, can I?" she asked as he tossed a bedroll into the back.

"I'm sorry," Brady said, remembering the woman's scream and fall beside him, blood blossoming on her back. His Julia wouldn't die that way. She would die in her own bed, in the luxury and comfort she was used to. He took her hands. "I don't want to be apart from you, but I don't know any other way."

She stroked his face. "We have to remember—" she said. The tears that lined the rims of her eyes didn't touch her voice. "—that this is the work that will make you great."

"You have already made me great," he said, and kissed her one final time.

1863

Brady pushed his blue-tinted glasses up on his nose and wiped the sweat off his brow with the back of his hand. The Pennsylvania sun beat on his long black waistcoat, baking his clothes against his skin. The corpse, only a few hours dead, was already gaseous and bloated, straining its frayed Union uniform. The too-florid smell of death ripened the air. If it weren't for the bodies, human and equine, the farmer's land would seem peaceful, not the site of one of the bloodiest battles of the war.

Brady tilted the corpse's head back. Underneath the gray mottled skin, a young boy's features had frozen in agony. Brady didn't have to alter the expression; he never did. The horror was always real. He set the repeating rifle lengthwise across the corpse, and stood up. A jagged row of posed corpses stretched before him. O'Sullivan had positioned the wagon toward the side of the field and was struggling with the tripod. Brady hurried to help his assistant, worried, always worried about destroying more equipment. They had lost so much trying to photograph the war. He should have known from the first battle how difficult this would be. He had sold nearly everything, asked Julia to give up even the simplest comforts, borrowed against his name from the Anthonys for equipment to record this. History. His country's folly and its glory. And the great, terrible waste of lives. He glanced back at the dead faces, wondered how many people would mourn.

"I think we should put it near the tree." O'Sullivan lugged the top half of the tripod at an angle away from the corpse row. "The light is good—the shade is on the other side. Mathew?"

"No." Brady backed up a few steps. "Here. See the angle? The bodies look random now, but you can see the faces."

He squinted, wishing he could see the faces better. His eyesight had been growing worse; in 1851 it had been so bad that the press thought he would be blind in a decade. Twelve years had passed and he wasn't blind yet. But he wasn't far from it.

O'Sullivan arranged the black curtain, then Brady swept his assistant aside. "Let me," he said.

He climbed under the curtain. The heat was thicker; the familiar scent of chemicals cleared the death from his nose. He peered through the lens. The image was as he had expected it to be, clear, concise, well composed. The light filtered through, reflected oddly through the blue tint on his glasses, and started a sharp ache in his skull. He pulled out, into the sun. "Adjust as you need to. But I think we have the image."

Brady turned away from the field as O'Sullivan prepared the wet plate and then shoved it into the camera. Sweat trickled down the back of Brady's neck into his woolen coat. He was tired, so tired, and the war had already lasted two years longer than anyone expected. He didn't know how many times he had looked on the faces of the dead, posed them for the camera the way he had posed princes and presidents a few years before. If he had stayed in New York, like the Anthonys, everything would have been different. He could have spent his nights with Julia...

"Got it," O'Sullivan said. He held the plate gingerly, his face flushed with the heat.

"You develop it," Brady said. "I want to stay here for a few minutes."

O'Sullivan frowned; Brady usually supervised every step of the battle images. But Brady didn't explain his unusual behavior. O'Sullivan said nothing. He clutched the plates and went in the back of the black-covered wagon. The wagon rocked ever so gently as he settled in.

27

Brady waited until the wagon stopped rocking, then clasped his hands behind his back and walked through the trampled, blood-spattered grass. The aftermath of battle made him restless: the dead bodies, the ruined earth, the shattered wagons. Battles terrified him, made him want to run screaming from the scene. He often clutched his equipment around him like a talisman—if he worked, if he didn't think about it, he would stave off the fear until the shooting stopped. He tripped over an abandoned canteen. He crouched, saw the bullet hole in its side.

"You stay, even though it appalls you."

The woman's voice startled him so badly he nearly screamed. He backed up as he stood, and found himself facing a thin, short-haired woman wearing pants, a short-sleeved shirt and (obviously) no undergarments. She looked familiar.

"That takes courage." She smiled. Her teeth were even and white.

"You shouldn't be here," he said. His voice shook and he clenched his fists to hide his shaking. "Are you looking for someone in particular? I can take you to the General."

"I'm looking for you. You're the man they call Brady of Broadway?"

He nodded.

"The man who sells everything, bargains his studio to photograph a war?"

Her comment was too close to his own thoughts—and

too personal. He felt a flush rise that had nothing to do with the heat. "What do you want?"

"I want you to work for me, Mathew Brady. I will pay for your equipment, take care of your travel, if you shoot pictures for me when and where I say."

She frightened him, a crazy woman standing in a field of dead men. "I run my own business," he said.

She nodded, the smile fading just a little. "And it will bankrupt you. You will die forgotten, your work hidden in crates in government warehouses. That's not why you do this, is it, Mr. Brady."

"I do this so that people can see what really happens here, so that people can travel through my memories to see this place," he said. The ache in his head grew sharper. This woman had no right to taunt him. "I do this for history."

"And it's history that calls you, Mr. Brady. The question is, will you serve?"

"I already serve," he snapped—and found himself speaking to air. Heat shimmered in front of him, distorting his view of the field for a moment. Then the tall grass and the broken picket fence returned, corpses hovering at the edge of his vision like bales of hay.

He took off his glasses and wiped his eyes. The strain was making him hallucinate. He had been too long in the sun. He would go back to the wagon, get a drink of water, lie in the shade. Then, perhaps, the memory of the hallucination would go away.

But her words haunted him as he retraced his steps. *I will pay for your equipment, take care of your travel.* If only someone would do that. He had spent the entire sum of his fortune and still saw no end ahead. She hadn't been a hallucination: she had been a dream. A wish for a different, easier life that no one would ever fulfill.

1865

The day after Appomattox—the end of the war, Brady dreamed:

He walked the halls of a well-lit place he had never seen before. His footsteps echoed on the shiny floor covering. Walls, made of a smooth material that was not wood or stone, smelled of paint and emollients. Ceiling boxes encased the lamps—and the light did not flicker but flowed cleaner than gaslight. Most of the doors lining the hallway were closed, but one stood open. A sign that shone with a light of its own read:

MATHEW B. BRADY EXHIBIT

OFFICIAL PHOTOGRAPHER:

UNITED STATES CIVIL WAR

(1861-1865)

Inside, he found a spacious room twice the size of any room he had ever seen, with skylights in the ceiling and Doric columns creating a hollow in the center. A camera, set up on its tripod, had its black curtain thrown half back, as if waiting for him to step inside. Next to it stood his wagon, looking out of place and ancient without its horse. The wagon's back door also stood open, and Brady saw the wooden boxes of plates inside, placed neatly, so that a path led to the darkroom. The darkroom looked odd: no one had picked up the sleeping pallets, and yet the chemical baths sat out, ready for use. He would never have left the wagon that way. He shook his head, and turned toward the rest of the room.

Three of the long, wide walls were bare. On the fourth, framed pictures crowded together. He walked to them, saw that they were his portraits, his work from Bull Run, Antietam, Gettysburg. He even saw a picture of General Lee in his confederate gray. Beneath the portrait, the attribution read *By Brady (or assistant)*, but Brady had never taken such a portrait, never developed one, never posed one. A chill ran up his back when he realized he hadn't squinted to read the print. He reached up, touched the bridge of his nose. His glasses were gone. He hadn't gone without glasses since he had been a boy. In the mornings, he had to grab his glasses off the nightstand first, then get out of bed.

His entire wartime collection (with huge gaps) framed, on exhibit. Four thousand portraits, displayed for the world to see, just as he had hoped. He reached out to the Lee portrait. As his finger brushed the smooth wood—

—he found himself beneath the large tree next to the Appomattox farmhouse, where the day before Lee and Grant had signed the peace treaty. The farmhouse was a big white blur against the blue of the April sky. He grabbed his glasses (somehow they had fallen to his lap) and hooked the frames around his ears. The world came into sharper focus, the bluetint easing the glare of the sun. He knew what he had to do. Even though he had arrived too late to photograph the historic signing of the treaty, he could still photograph General Lee one last time in his uniform.

Brady got up and brushed the grass off his pants. His wagon stood beside the farmhouse. The wagon looked proper—dust-covered, mud-spattered, with a few splintered boards and a cock-eyed wheel that he would have to fix very soon—not clean and neat as it had in his dream. The horse, tied to another tree, looked tired, but he would push her with him to Richmond, to General Lee, to complete the exhibit.

Three empty walls, he thought as he went to find his assistant. He wondered why his earlier portraits weren't mounted there. Perhaps the walls awaited something else. Something better.

1866

Brady held his nephew Levin's shoulders and propelled him toward the door. The ticket taker at the desk in the lobby of the New York Historical Society waved them past.

"How many today, John?" Brady asked.

"We had a few paying customers yesterday," the large man said, "but they all left after looking at the first wall."

Brady nodded. The society had said they would close the exhibit of his war portraits if attendance didn't go up. But despite the free publicity in the illustrated newspapers and the positive critical response, the public was not attending.

Levin had already gone inside. He stood, hands behind his back, and stared at the portraits of destruction he had been too young to remember. Brady had brought Levin to the exhibit to discourage the boy and make him return to school. He had arrived a few days before, declaring that he wanted to be a photographer like his Uncle Mat. Brady had said twelve was too young to start learning the trade, but Julia had promised Levin a place to stay if no one demanded that he return to school. So far, no one had.

Brady went inside too. The lighting was poor, and the portraits were scattered on several small walls. No Doric columns, no wide empty spaces. This was a cramped showing, like so many others he had had, but it shared the emptiness of the gallery in his dreams.

He stared at the portraits, knowing them by heart. They ran in order, from the first glorious parade down Pennsylvania Avenue—taken from his Washington studio—to the last portrait of Lee after Appomattox. Each portrait took him back to the sights and sounds of the moment: the excitement of the parade, the disgust at the carnage, the hopelessness in Lee's eyes. It was here: the recent past, recorded as faithfully as a human being could. One of his reviewers had said that Brady had captured time and held it prisoner in his little glass plates. He certainly did in his mind. Sometimes all it took was a smell—decaying garbage, horse sweat—and he was back on the battlefield, fighting to live while he took his portraits.

From outside the door, he heard the murmur of voices. He turned in time to see John talking to a woman in widow's weeds. John pointed at Brady. Brady smiled and nodded, knowing he was being identified as the artist behind the exhibit.

The woman pushed open the glass doors and stood in front of Brady. She was slight and older than he expected—in her forties or fifties—with deep lines around her eyes and the corners of her mouth.

"I've come to plead with you, Mr. Brady," she said. Her voice was soft. "I want you to take these portraits away. Over there, you have an image of my husband's body, and in the next room, I saw my son. They're dead, Mr. Brady, and I buried them. I want to think about how they lived, not how they died."

"I'm sorry, ma'am," Brady said. He didn't turn to see which portraits she had indicated. "I didn't mean to offend you. These portraits show what war really is, and I think it's something we need to remember lest we try it again."

Levin had stopped his movement through the gallery. He hadn't turned toward the conversation, but Brady could tell the boy was listening from the cocked position of his head.

"We'll remember, Mr. Brady," the woman said. She smoothed her black skirt. "My whole family has no choice."

She turned her back and walked out, her steps firm and proud. The street door closed sharply behind her. John got up from his chair.

"You've gotten this before," Brady said.

"Every day," John said. "People want to move forward, Mathew. They don't need more reminders of the past."

Brady glanced at his nephew. Levin had moved into one of the back rooms. "Once Levin is done looking at the exhibit, I'll help you remove it," Brady said. "No sense hurting your business to help mine."

He sighed and glanced around the room. Four years of work. Injured associates, ruined equipment, lost wealth, and a damaged business. He had expected acclaim, at least, if not a measure of additional fame. One of his mother's aphorisms rose in his mind: a comment she used to make when he would come inside, covered with dirt and dung. "How the mighty hath fallen," she'd say. She had never appreciated his dreams nor had she lived long enough to see them come true. Now her shade stood beside him, as clearly as she had stood on the porch so many years ago, and he could hear the "I-told-you-so" in her voice.

He shook the apparition away. What his mother had never realized was that the mighty had farther to fall.

1871

That morning, he put on his finest coat, his best hat, and he kissed Julia with a passion he hadn't shown in years. She smiled at him, her eyes filled with tears, as she held the door open for him. He stepped into the hallway, and heard the latch snick shut behind him. Nothing looked different: the gas lamps had soot marks around the base of the chimneys; the flowered wallpaper peeled in one corner; the stairs creaked as he stepped on them, heading down to the first floor and the street. Only he felt different: the shuddery bubble in his stomach, the tension in his back, the lightheadedness threatening the sureness of his movements.

He stopped on the first landing and took a breath of the musty hotel air. He wondered what they would think of him now, all the great men he had known. They came back to him, like battlefield ghosts haunting a general. Samuel Morse, his large dark eyes snapping, his gnarled hands holding the daguerreotypes, his voice echoing in the room, teaching Brady that photography would cause a revolution —a revolution, boy!—and he had to ride the crest.

"I did," Brady whispered. His New York studio, so impressive in the 1850s, had a portrait of Morse hanging near the door for luck. Abraham Lincoln had gazed at that portrait. So had his assassin, John Wilkes Booth. Presidents, princes, actors, assassins had all passed through Brady's door. And he, in his arrogance, had thought his work art, not commerce. Art and history demanded his presence at the first Battle of Bull Run. Commerce had demanded he stay home, take *carte de visites*, imperials, and portraits of soldiers going off to war, of families about to be destroyed, of politicians, great and small.

No. He had left his assistants to do that, while he spent their earnings, his fortune, and his future chasing a dream.

And this morning, he would pay for that dream.

So simple, his attorney told him. He would sign his name to a paper, declare bankruptcy, and the government would apportion his assets to his remaining creditors. He could still practice his craft, still attempt to repay his debts, still *live*, if someone wanted to call that living.

He adjusted his jacket one final time and stepped into the hotel's lobby. The desk clerk called out his customary good morning, and Brady nodded. He would show no shame, no anger. The doorman opened the door and cool, manure-tinged air tickled Brady's nostrils. He took a deep breath and walked into the bustle of the morning: Mathew Brady, photographer. A man who had joked with Andrew Jackson, Martin Van Buren, and James Buchanan. A man who had raised a camera against bullets, who had held more dead and dying than half the physicians on the battlefield. Brady pushed forward, touching the brim of his hat each time he passed a woman, nodding at the gentlemen as if the day were the best in his life. Almost everyone had seen his work, in the illustrated papers, in the exhibits, in the halls of Congress itself. He had probably photographed the sons of most of the people who walked these streets. Dead faces, turned toward the sun.

The thought sobered him. These people had lost husbands, fathers, children. Losses greater than his. And they had survived, somehow. Somehow.

He held the thought as he made his way through the morning, listening to the attorney mumble, the government officials drone on, parceling out his possessions like clothing at an orphan's charity. The thought carried him out the door, and back onto the street before the anger burst through the numbness:

The portraits were his children. He and Julia had none —and he had nothing else. Nothing else at all.

"Now, are you ready to work with me?"

The female voice was familiar enough that he knew

who he would see before he looked up: the crazy woman who haunted him, who wanted him to give everything he could to history.

As if he hadn't given enough.

She stood before him, the winter sunlight backlighting her and hiding her features in shadow. The Washington crowd walked around her, unseeing, as if she were no more than a post blocking the path.

"And what do I get if I help you?" he asked, his voice sounding harsher than he had ever heard it.

"Notice. Acclaim. Pictures on walls instead of buried in warehouses. The chance to make a very real difference."

He glanced back at the dark wooden door, at the moving figures faint in the window, people who had buried his art, given it to the Anthonys, separated it and segregated it and declared it worthless. His children, as dead as the ones he had photographed.

"And you'll pay my way?" he asked.

"I will provide your equipment and handle your travel, if you take photographs for me when and where I say."

"Done," he said, extending a hand to seal the bargain, thinking a crazy, mannish woman like this one would close a deal like a gentleman. She took his hand, her palm soft, unused to work, and as she shook, the world whirled. Colors and pain and dust bombarded him. Smells he would briefly catch and by the time he identified them disappeared. His head ached, his eyes throbbed, his body felt as if it were being torn in fifteen different directions. And when they stopped, he was in a world of blackness, where hot rain fell like fire from the sky.

"I need you to photograph this," she said, and then she disappeared. In her place, his wagon stood, the only friend in a place of strangeness. The air smelled of burning buildings, of sticky wet, of decay. Death. He recognized it from the battlefields years ago. The horizon was black, dotted with orange flame. The trees rose stunted against the oppression. People—Orientals, he realized with some amazement—ran by him, their strange clothing ripped and torn, their faces burned, peeling, shining with the strange heat. They made no sound as they moved: all he heard was the rain slapping against the road.

He grabbed an old man, stopped him, felt the soft, decaying flesh dissolve between his fingers. "What is this place?" he asked.

The old man reached out a trembling hand, touched Brady's round eyes, his white skin. "American—" the old man took a deep breath and exhaled into a wail that became a scream. He wrenched his arm from Brady's grasp, and started to run. The people around him screamed too, and ran, as if they were fleeing an unseen enemy. Brady grabbed his wagon, rocking with the force of the panicked crowd, and hurried to the far side.

People lay across the grass like corpses on the battlefield. Only these corpses moved. A naked woman swayed in the middle of the ground, her body covered with burns except for large flower-shaped patches all over her torso. And beside him lay three people, their faces melted away, their eyes bubbling holes in their smooth, shiny faces.

"What is this?" he cried out again.

But the woman who had brought him here was gone.

One of the faceless people grabbed his leg. He shook the hand away, trembling with the horror. The rich smell of decay made him want to gag.

He had been in this situation before—in the panic, among the decay, in the death—and he had found only one solution.

He reached inside his wagon and pulled out the camera. This time, though, he didn't scout for artistic composition. He turned the lens on the field of corpses, more horrifying than anything he'd seen under the Pennsylvania sun, and took portrait after portrait after portrait, building an artificial wall of light and shadow between himself and the black rain, the foul stench, and the silent, grasping hands of hundreds of dying people.

1871

And hours—or was it days?—later, after he could no longer move the tripod alone, no longer hold a plate between his fingers, after she appeared and took his wet plates and his equipment and his wagon, after he had given water to more people than he could count, and tore his suit and felt the sooty rain drops dig into his skin, after all that, he found himself standing on the same street in Washington, under the same sunlit winter sky. A woman he had never seen before peered at him with concern on her wrinkled face and asked, "Are you all right, sir?"

"I'm fine," he said and felt the lightheadedness that had threatened all morning take him to his knees on the wooden sidewalk. People surrounded him and someone called him by name. They took his arms and half carried him to the hotel. He dimly realized that they got him up the stairs—the scent of lilacs announcing Julia's presence—and onto the bed. Julia's cool hand rested against his forehead and her voice, murmuring something soothing, washed over him like a blessing. He closed his eyes—

And dreamed in jumbled images:

Flowers burned into naked skin; row after row after row of bodies stretched out in a farmer's field, face after face tilted toward the sun; and the faces blend into troops marching under gray skies, General Grant's dust-covered voice repeating that war needs different rules, different players, and General Lee, staring across a porch on a gray April morning, wearing his uniform for the last time, saying softly that being a soldier is no longer an occupation for gentlemen. And through it all, black rain fell from the gray skies, coating everything in slimy heat, burning through skin, leaving bodies ravaged, melting people's clothes from their frames—

Brady gasped and sat up. Julia put her arm around him. "It's all right, Mathew," she said. "You were dreaming."

He put his head on her shoulder, and closed his eyes. Immediately, flower-burned skin rose in his vision and he forced his eyelids open. He still wore his suit, but there was no long gash in it and the fabric was dry. "I don't know what's wrong with me," he said.

"You just need rest."

He shook his head and got up. His legs were shaky, but

the movement felt good. "Think of where we would be if I hadn't gone to Bull Run," he said. "We were rich. We had what we wanted. I would have taken portraits, and we would have made more money. We would have an even nicer studio and a home, instead of this apartment." He smiled a little. "And now the government will sell everything they can, except the portraits. Portraits that no one wants to see."

Julia still sat at the edge of the bed. Her black dress was wrinkled, and her ringlets mussed. She must have held him while he slept.

"You know," he said, leaning against the windowsill, "I met a woman just after the Battle of Gettysburg, and she told me that I would die forgotten with my work hidden in government warehouses. And I thought she was crazy; how could the world forget Brady of Broadway? I had dreams of a huge gallery, filled with my work—"

"Dreams have truth," Julia said.

"No," Mathew said. "Dreams have hope. Dreams without hope are nightmares." He swept his hand around the room. "This is a nightmare, Julia."

She bowed her head. Her hands were clasped together so tightly her knuckles had turned white. Then she raised her head, tossing her ringlets back, and he saw the proud young woman he had married. "So how do we change things, Mathew?"

He stared at her. Even now, she still believed in him,

thought that together they could make things better. He wanted to tell her that they would recapture what they had lost; he wanted to give her hope. But he was forty-eight years old, nearly blind, and penniless. He didn't have time to rebuild a life from nothing.

"I guess we keep working," he said, quietly. But even as he spoke, a chill ran down his back. He had worked for the crazy woman and she had taken him to the gates of hell. And he had nothing to show for it except strange behavior and frightening memories. "I'm sorry, Julia."

"I'm not." She smiled that cryptic smile she had had ever since he married her. "The reward is worth the cost."

He nodded, feeling the rain still hot on his skin, hearing voices call for help in a language he could not understand. He wondered if any reward was worth the sacrifices made for it.

He didn't think so.

1871

S ix weeks later, Brady dreamed:

The exhibit room was colder than it had been before, the lighting better. Brady stood beside his wagon and clutched its wooden frame. He stepped around the wagon, saw that the doors to the exhibit were closed, and he was alone in the huge room. He touched his eyes. The glasses were missing, and he could see, just as he had in the previous dreams. His vision was clear, clearer than it had ever been.

No portraits had been added to the far wall. He walked toward his collection and then stopped. He didn't want to look at his old work. He couldn't bear the sight of it, knowing the kind of pain and loss those portraits had caused. Instead he turned and gasped.

Portraits graced a once-empty wall. He ran toward

them, nearly tripping over the boards of the wagon. Hundreds of portraits framed and mounted at odd angles glinted under the strange directed lights, the lights that never flickered. He stood closer, saw scenes he hoped he would forget: the flowered woman; the three faceless people, their eyes boiling in their sockets; a weeping man, his skin hanging around him like rags. The portraits were clearer, cleaner than the war portraits from the other wall. No dust had gotten in the fluid, no cracked wet plates, no destroyed glass. Clean, crisp portraits, on paper he had never seen before. But it was all his work, clearly his work.

He made himself look away. The air had a metallic smell. The rest of the wall was blank, as were the other two. More pictures to take, more of hell to see. He had experienced the fire and the brimstone, the burning rain— Satan's tears. He wondered what else he would see, what else she would make him record.

He touched the portrait of the men with melted faces. If he had to trade visions like this for his eyesight and his wealth, he wouldn't make the trade. He would die poor and blind at Julia's side.

The air got colder.

He woke up screaming.

1873

Brady stared at the plate he held in his hand. His subject had long since left the studio, but Brady hadn't moved. He remembered days when subject after subject had entered the studio, and his assistants had had to develop the prints while Brady staged the sittings.

"I'll take that, Uncle."

Brady started. He hadn't realized that Levin was in the room. He wondered if Levin had been watching Brady stand there, doing nothing. Levin hadn't said anything the past few years, but he seemed to notice Brady's growing strange behaviors. "Thank you, Levin," Brady said, making sure his voice was calm.

Levin kept his eyes averted as he grabbed the covered plate and took it into the darkroom for developing. Levin had grown tall in the seven years that he'd been with Brady. Far from the self-assured twelve-year-old who had come to work for his uncle, Levin had become a silent man who came alive only behind the camera lens. Brady couldn't have survived without him, especially after he had to let the rest of his staff go.

Brady moved the camera, poured the collodion mixture back into its jar, and covered the silver nitrate. Then he washed his hands in the bowl filled with tepid water that sat near the chemical storage.

"I have another job for you. Can you be alone on Friday at four?"

This time, Brady didn't jump, but his heart did. It pounded against his ribcage like a child trying to escape a locked room. His nerves had been on edge for so long. Julia kept giving him hot teas and rubbing the back of his neck, but nothing seemed to work. When he closed his eyes he saw visions he didn't want to see.

He turned, slowly. The crazy woman stood there, her hands clasped behind her back. Since she hadn't appeared in almost two years, he had managed to convince himself that she wasn't real—that he had imagined her.

"Another job?" he asked. He was shaking. Either he hadn't imagined the last one, or he was having another nightmare. "I'm sorry. I can't."

"Can't?" Her cheeks flushed. "You promised, Mathew. I need you."

"You never told me you were going to send me to hell," he snapped. He moved away from the chemicals, afraid that in his anger, he would throw them. "You're not real, and yet the place you took me stays in my mind. I'm going crazy. You're a sign of my insanity."

"No," she said. She came forward and touched him lightly. Her fingertips were soft, and he could smell the faint perfume of her body. "You're not crazy. You're just faced with something from outside your experience. You had dreams about the late War, didn't you? Visions you couldn't escape?"

He was about to deny it, when he remembered how, in the first year of his return, the smell of rotted garbage took him back to the Devil's Hole; how the whinny of a horse made him duck for cover; how he stored his wagon because being inside it filled him with a deep anxiety. "What are you telling me?"

"I come from a place you've never heard of," she said. "We have developed the art of travel in an instant and our societal norms are different from yours. The place I sent you wasn't hell. It was a war zone, after the Uni—a country had used a new kind of weapon on another country. I want to send you to more places like that, to photograph them, so that we can display those photographs for people of my society to see."

"If you can travel in an instant—" and he remembered the whirling world, the dancing colors and sounds as he traveled from his world to another "—then why don't you take people there? Why do you need me?"

"Those places are forbidden. I received special dispensation. I'm working on an art project, and I nearly lost my funding because I saw you in Gettysburg."

Brady's shaking eased. "You risked everything to see me?"

She nodded. "We're alike in that way," she said. "You've risked everything to follow your vision too."

"And you need me?"

"You're the first and the best, Mathew. I couldn't even get funding unless I guaranteed that I would have your work. Your studio portraits are lovely, Mathew, but it's your war photos that make you great."

"No one wants to see my war work," Brady said.

Her smile seemed sad. "They will, Mathew. Especially if you work with me."

Brady glanced around his studio, smaller now than it had ever been. Portraits of great men still hung on the walls along with actors, artists, and people who just wanted a remembrance.

"At first it was art for you," she said, her voice husky. "Then it became a mission, to show people what war was really like. And now no one wants to look. But they need to, Mathew."

"I know," he said. He glanced back at her, saw the brightness in her face, the trembling of her lower lip. This meant more to her than an art project should. Something personal, something deep, got her involved. "I went to hell for you, and I never even got to see the results of my work."

"Yes, you did," she said.

"Uncle!" Levin called from the next room.

The woman vanished, leaving shimmering air in her wake. Brady reached out and touched it, felt the remains of a whirlwind. She knew about his dreams, then. Or was she referring to the work he had done inside his wagon on the site, developing plates before they dried so that the portraits would be preserved?

"Did I hear voices?" Levin came out of the back room, wiping his hands on his smock.

Brady glanced at Levin, saw the frown between the young man's brows. Levin was really worried about him. "No voices," Brady said. "Perhaps you just heard someone calling from the street."

"The portrait is done." Levin looked at the chemicals, as if double-checking his uncle's work.

"I'll look at it later," Brady said. "I'm going home to Julia. Can you watch the studio?"

Levin nodded.

Brady grabbed his coat off one of the sitting chairs and stopped at the doorway. "What do you think of my war work, Levin? And be honest, now."

"Honest?"

"Yes."

Brady waited. Levin took a deep breath. "I wish that I were ten years older so that I could have been one of your assistants, Uncle. You preserved something that future generations need to see. And it angers me that no one is willing to look."

"Me, too," Brady said. He slipped his arms through the sleeves of his coat. "But maybe—" and he felt something cautious rise in his chest, something like hope, "—if I work just a little harder, people will look again. Think so, Levin?"

"It's one of my prayers, Uncle," Levin said.

"Mine, too," Brady said and let himself out the door. He whistled a little as he walked down the stairs. Maybe the woman was right; maybe he had a future, after all.

1873

Friday at four, Brady whirled from his studio to a place so hot that sweat appeared on his body the instant he stopped whirling. His wagon stood on a dirt road, surrounded by thatched huts. Some of the huts were burning, but the flames were the only movement in the entire village. Far away, he could hear a chop-chop-chopping sound, but he could see nothing. Flies buzzed around him, not landing, as if they had more interesting places to go. The air smelled of burning hay and something fetid, something familiar. He swallowed and looked for the bodies.

He grabbed the back end of the wagon, and climbed inside. The darkness was welcome. It took a moment for his eyes to get used to the gloom, then he grabbed his tripod and his camera and carried them outside. He pushed his glasses up his nose, but his finger encountered skin instead of metal. He could see. He squinted and wondered how she did that—gave him his eyesight for such a short period of time. Perhaps it was his reward for going to hell.

A hand extended from one of the burning huts. Brady stopped beside it, crouched, and saw a man lying facedown in the dust, the back of his head blown away. Bile rose in Brady's throat, and he swallowed to keep his last meal down. He assembled the camera, uncapped the lens, and looked through, seeing the hand and the flames flickering in his narrow, rounded vision. Then he climbed out from under the curtain, went back into the wagon, and prepared a plate.

This time he felt no fear. Perhaps knowing that the woman (why had she never told him her name?) could flash him out of the area in an instant made him feel safer. Or perhaps it was his sense of purpose, as strong as it had been at the first battle of Bull Run, when the bullets whizzed by him, and his wagon got stampeded by running soldiers. He had had a reason then, a life then, and he would get it back.

He went outside and photographed the dead man in the burning hut. The chop-chop-chopping sound was fading, but he heat seemed to intensify. The stillness in the village was eerie. The crackles of burning buildings made him jump. He saw no more bodies, no evidence other than the emptiness and the fires that something had happened in this place.

Then he saw the baby.

It was a toddler, actually. Naked, and shot in the back, the body lying at the edge of a ditch. Brady walked over to the ditch and peered in, then stepped back and got sick for the first time in his professional career.

Bodies filled the ditch—women, children, babies, and old men—their limbs flung back, stomachs gone, faces shot away. Blood flowed like a river, added its coppery scent to the smell of burning hay and the reek of decay. What kind of places was she taking him to, where women and children died instead of soldiers?

He grabbed his camera, his shield, and set it up, knowing that this would haunt him as the hot, slimy rain haunted him. He prepared more plates and photographed the toddler over and over, the innocent baby that had tried to crawl away from the horror and had been shot in the back for its attempts at survival.

And as he worked, his vision blurred, and he wondered why the sweat pouring into and out of his eyes never made them burn.

1875

Brady stared at the $25,000 check. He set it on the doily that covered the end table. In the front room, he heard Levin arguing with Julia.

"Not today," she said. "Give him at least a breath between bad news."

Brady touched the thin paper, the flowing script. The government had given him one-quarter of the wealth he had lost going into the war, one-tenth of the money he spent photographing history. And too late. The check was too late. A month earlier, the War Department, which owned the title to the wet plates, sold them all to the Anthonys for an undisclosed sum. They had clear, legal title, and Edward Anthony had told Brady that they would never, ever sell.

He got up with a sigh and brushed aside the half-open bedroom door. "Tell me what?" he asked.

Levin looked up—guiltily, Brady thought. Julia hid something behind her back. "Nothing, Uncle," Levin said. "It can wait."

"You brought something and I want to know what it is." Brady's voice was harsh. It had been too harsh lately. The flashbacks on his travels, the strain of keeping silent —of not telling Julia the fantastical events—and the reversal after reversal in his own life were taking their toll.

Julia brought her hand out from behind her back. She clutched a stereoscope. The small device shook as she handed it to Brady.

He put the lenses up to his eyes, feeling the frame clink against his glasses. The three dimensional view inside was familiar: The war parade he had taken over ten years ago, as the soldiers rode down Pennsylvania Avenue. Brady removed the thick card from the viewer. The two portraits stood side by side, as he expected. He even expected the flowery script on the side, stating that the stereoscopic portrait was available through the Anthonys' warehouse. What he didn't expect wad the attribution at the bottom, claiming that the photography had been done by the Anthonys themselves.

He clenched his fists and turned around, letting the device fall to the wooden floor. The stereoscope clinked as it rolled, and Brady stifled an urge to kick it across the room.

"We can go to Congressman Garfield," Levin said, "and maybe he'll help us."

Brady stared at the portrait. He could take the Anthonys to court. They did own the rights to the wet plates, but they should have given him proper attribution. It seemed a trivial thing to fight over. He had no money, and what influence he had would be better spent getting the plates back than fighting for a bit of name recognition. "No," Brady said. "You can go to the newspapers, if you like, Levin, but we won't get James to act for us. He's done his best already. This is our fight. And we'll keep at it, until the bitter end if we have to."

Julia clenched her hands together and stared at him. It seemed as if the lines around her mouth had grown deeper. He remembered the first time he danced with her, the diamonds around her neck glittering in the candlelight. They had sold those diamonds in 1864 to fund the Petersburg expedition—the expedition in which half of his equipment was destroyed by Confederate shells. *You are going to be a great man,* she had told him. The problem was, he had never asked her what she meant by great. Perhaps she thought of her wealthy father as a great man. Perhaps she stayed with Brady out of wifely loyalty.

She came over to him and put her arm around him. "I love you Mathew," she said. He hugged her close, so close that he worried he would hurt her. None of his work, none of his efforts would have been possible—especially in the lean years—if she hadn't believed in him.

"I'm sorry," he whispered into her shoulder.

She slipped out of his embrace and held him so that she could look into his eyes. "We'll keep fighting, Mathew. And in the end, we'll win."

1877

And the assignments kept coming. Brady began to look forward to the whirling, even though he often ended up in hell. His body was stronger there; his eyesight keener. He could forget, for a short time, the drabness of Washington, the emptiness of his life. On the battlefields, he worked—and he could still believe that his work had meaning.

One dark, gray day, he left his studio and found himself hiding at the edge of a forest. His wagon, without a horse, leaned against a spindly tree. The air was thick and humid. Brady's black suit clung to his skin, already damp. Through the bushes he could see soldiers carrying large rifles, surrounding a church. Speaking a language he thought he understood—Spanish?—they herded children together.

Then, in twos and threes, the soldiers marched the children inside.

The scene was eerily quiet. Brady went behind the wagon, grabbed his tripod, and set up the camera. He stepped carefully on the forest bed; the scuffling noise of his heavy leather shoes seemed to resound like gunshots. He took portrait after portrait, concentrating on the soldiers' faces, the children's looks of resignation. He wondered why the soldiers were imprisoning the children, and what they planned to do to the town he could see just over the horizon. And a small trickle of relief ran through him that here, at least, the children would be spared.

Once the children were inside, the soldiers closed the heavy doors and barred them. Someone had already boarded up the windows. Brady put another plate into his camera to take a final portrait of the closed church before following the army to their nasty work at the village. He looked down, checking the plates the woman had given him, when he heard a whoosh. A sharp, tingling scent rose in his nostrils, followed by the smell of smoke. Automatically he opened the lens—just as a soldier threw a burning torch at the church itself.

Brady screamed and ran out of the bushes. The soldiers saw him—and one leveled a rifle at him. The bullets ratt-a-tatted at him, the sound faster and more vicious than the repeating rifles from the war. Brady felt his body jerk and fall, felt himself roll over, bouncing with each bullet's

impact. He wanted to crawl to the church, to save the children, but he couldn't move. He couldn't do anything. The
world was growing darker—and he saw a kind of light—
and his mother? waiting for him—

And then the whirling began. It seemed slower, and he
wasn't sure he wanted it to start. It pulled him away from
the light, away from the mother he hadn't seen since he left
the farm at 16, away from the church and the burning children (he thought he could hear their screams now—loud,
terrified, piercing—) and back to the silence of his studio.

He wound up in one of his straight-backed chairs. He
tried to stand up, and fell, his glasses jostling the edge of
his nose. Footsteps on the stairs ran toward him, then
hands lifted him. Levin.

"Uncle? Are you all right?"

"Shot," Brady whispered. "The children. All dead. Must
get the children."

He pushed Levin aside and groped for something,
anything to hold on to. "I have to get back!" he yelled.
"Someone has to rescue those children!"

Levin grabbed his shoulders, forced Brady back to the
chair. "The war is over, Uncle," Levin said. "It's over. You're
home. You're safe."

Brady looked up at Levin and felt the shakes begin. She
wouldn't send him back. She wouldn't let him save those
children. She knew all along that the church would burn
and she wanted him to photograph it, to record it, not to

save it. He put his hands over his face. He had seen enough atrocities to last him three lifetimes.

"It's all right," Levin said. "It's all right, Uncle."

It wasn't all right. Levin was becoming an expert at this, at talking Brady home. And to his credit, he never said anything to Julia. "Thank you," Brady said. His words were thin, rushed, as if the bullet holes still riddled his body and sucked the air from it.

He patted Levin on the shoulder, then walked away—walked—to the end of the studio, his room, his home. Perhaps the crazy woman didn't exist. Perhaps what Levin saw was truth. Perhaps Brady's mind was going, after all.

"Thank you," he repeated, and walked down the stairs, comforted by the aches in his bones, the blurry edge to his vision. He was home, and he would stay—

Until she called him again. Until he had his next chance to be young, and working, and doing something worthwhile.

1882

Brady sat in front of the window, gazing into the street. Below, carriages rumbled past, throwing up mud and chunks of ice. People hurried across the sidewalk, heads bowed against the sleet. The rippled glass was cold against his fingers, but he didn't care. He could hear Levin in the studio, talking with a prospective client. Levin had handled all of the business this past week. Brady had hardly been able to move.

The death of Henry Anthony shouldn't have hit him so hard. The Anthony Brothers had been the closest thing Brady had to enemies in the years since the war. Yet, they had been friends once, and companions in the early days of the art. All of photography was dying. Morse was gone. Henry Anthony dead. And three of Brady's assistants, men he had trained to succeed him, dead in the opening of the West.

Levin opened the door and peeked in. "Uncle, a visitor," he said.

Brady was about to wave Levin away when another man stepped inside. The man was tall, gaunt, wearing a neatly pressed black suit. He looked official. "Mr. Brady?"

Brady nodded but did not rise.

"I'm John C. Taylor. I'm a soldier, sir, and a student of your work. I would like to talk with you, if I could."

Brady pushed back the needlepoint chair beside him. Taylor sat down, hat in his hands.

"Mr. Brady, I wanted to let you know what I've been doing. Since the end of the war, I've tried to acquire your work. I have secured, through various channels, over 7,000 negatives of your best pictures."

Brady felt the haze that surrounded him lift somewhat. "And you would like to display them?"

"No, sir, actually, I've been trying to preserve them. The plates the government bought from you years ago have been sitting in a warehouse. A number were destroyed due to incautious handling. I've been trying to get them placed somewhere else. I have an offer from the Navy Department—I have connections there—and I wanted your approval."

Brady laughed. The sound bubbled from inside of him, but he felt no joy. He had wanted the portraits for so long and finally, here was someone asking for his approval. "No one has asked me what I wanted before."

Taylor leaned back. He glanced once at Levin, as if Brady's odd reaction had made Taylor wary.

"My uncle has gone through quite an odyssey to hold on to his plates," Levin said softly. "He has lost a lot over the years."

"From the beginning," Brady said. "No one will ever know what I went through in securing the negatives. The whole world can never appreciate it. It changed the course of my life. Some of those negatives nearly cost me that life. And then the work was taken from me. Do you understand, Mr. Taylor?"

Taylor nodded. "I've been tracking these photographs for a long time, sir. I remembered them from the illustrated papers, and I decided that they needed to be preserved, so that my children's children would see the devastation, would learn the follies we committed because we couldn't reason with each other."

Bray smiled. A man who did understand. Finally. "The government bought my portraits of Webster, Calhoun, and Clay. I got paid a lot of money for those paintings that were made from my photographs. Not my work, mind you. Paintings of my work. Page would have been so happy."

"Sir?"

Brady shook his head. Page had left his side long ago. "But no one wants to see the war work. No one wants to see what you and I preserved. I don't want the Navy to bury the negatives. I want them to display the work, reproduce it or make it into a book that someone can see."

"First things first, Mr. Brady," Taylor said. "The Navy has the negatives I've acquired, but we need to remove the others from the War Department before they're destroyed. And then you, or your nephew, or someone else can go in there and put together a showing."

Brady reached over and gripped Taylor's hands. They were firm and strong—a young man's hands on an older man's body. "If you can do that," Brady said, "You will have made all that I've done worthwhile."

1882

Julia huddled on the settee, a blanket over her slight frame. She had grown gaunt, her eyes big saucers on the planes of her face. Her hands shook as she took the letter from Brady. He had hesitated about giving it to her, but he knew that she would ask and she would worry. It would be better for her frail heart to know than to constantly fret. She leaned toward the lamp. Brady watched her eyes move as she read.

He already knew the words by heart. The letter was from General A. W. Greeley, in the War Department. He was in charge of the government's collection of Brady's work. After the opening amenities, he had written:

The government has stated positively that their negatives must not be exploited for commercial purposes. They are the historical treasures of a whole people and the government has justly refused to establish a dangerous system of "special privilege" by granting permission for publication to individuals. As the property of the people, the government negatives are held in sacred trust...

Where no one could see them, and not even Brady himself could use them. He wondered what Taylor thought —Taylor, who would have received the letter in Connecticut by now.

Julia looked up, her eyes dotted with tears. "What do they think, that you're going to steal the plates from them like they stole them from you?"

"I don't know," Brady said. "Perhaps they really don't understand what they have."

"They understand," Julia said, her voice harsh. "And it frightens them."

1883

I n his dreams, he heard the sounds of people working. Twice he had arrived at the door to his gallery, and twice it had been locked. Behind the thin material, he heard voices—"Here, Andre. No, no. Keep the same years on the same wall space"—and the sounds of shuffling feet. This time, he knocked and the door opened a crack.

Ceiling lights flooded the room. It was wide and bright —brighter than he imagined a room could be. His work covered all the walls but one. People, dressed in pants and loose shirts like the woman who hired him, carried framed portraits from one spot to the next, all under the direction of a slim man who stood next to Brady's wagon.

The man looked at Brady. "What do you want?"

"I just wanted to see—"

The man turned to one of the others walking through. "Get rid of him, will you? We only have a few hours, and we still have one wall to fill."

A woman stopped next to Brady and put her hand on his arm. Her fingers were cool. "I'm sorry," she said. "We're preparing an exhibit."

"But I'm the artist," Brady said.

"He says—"

"I know what he says," the man said. He squinted at Brady, then glanced at a portrait that hung near the wagon. "And so he is. You should be finishing the exhibit, Mr. Brady, no gawking around the studio."

"I didn't know I had something to finish."

The man sighed. "The show opens tomorrow morning, and you still have one wall to fill. What are you doing here?"

"I don't know," Brady said. The woman took his arm and led him out the door.

"We'll see you tomorrow night," she said. And then she smiled. "I like your work."

And then he woke up, shivering and shaking in the dark beside Julia. Her even breathing was a comfort. He drew himself into a huddle and rested his knees against his chest. One wall to fill by tomorrow? He wished he understood what the dreams meant. It had taken him nearly twenty years to fill all the other walls. And then he thought that perhaps dream time worked differently than real time. Perhaps dream time moved in an instant the way he did when the woman whirled him away to another place.

It was just a dream, he told himself, and by the time he fell back to sleep, he really believed it.

1884

By the time the wagon appeared beside him, Brady was shaking. This place was silent, completely silent. Houses stood in neat rows on barren, brown, treeless land. Their white formations rested like sentries against the mountains that stood in the distance. A faint smell, almost acrid, covered everything. The air was warm, but not muggy, and beads of sweat rose on his arms like drops of blood.

Brady had arrived behind one of the houses. Inside, a family sat around the table—a man, a woman, and two children. They all appeared to be eating—the woman had a spoon raised to her mouth—but no one moved. In the entire time he had been there, no one had moved.

He went into his wagon, removed the camera and tripod, then knocked on the door. The family didn't acknowledge him. He pushed the door open and stepped inside, setting up the camera near a gleaming countertop. Then he walked over to the family. The children were laughing, gazing at each other. Their chests didn't rise and fall, their eyes didn't move. The man had his hand around a cup full of congealed liquid. He was watching the children, a faint smile on his face. The woman was looking down, at the bowl filled with a soggy mush. The hand holding the spoon—empty except for a white stain in the center—had frozen near her mouth. Brady touched her. Her skin was cold, rigid.

They were dead.

Brady backed away, nearly knocking over the tripod. He grabbed the camera, felt its firmness in his hands. For some reason, these specters frightened him worse than all the others. He couldn't tell what killed them or how they died. It had become increasingly difficult, at the many varied places he had been, but he could at least guess. Here, he saw nothing—and the bodies didn't even feel real.

He climbed under the dark curtain, finding a kind of protection from his own equipment. Perhaps, near his own stuff, whatever had killed them would avoid him. He took the photograph, and then carried his equipment to the next house, where a frozen woman sat on a sofa, looking at a piece of paper. In each house, he took the still lifes, almost wishing for the blood, the fires, the signs of destruction.

1885

Brady folded the newspaper and set it down. He didn't wish to disturb Julia, who was sleeping soundly on the bed. She seemed to get so little rest. Her face had become translucent, the shadows under her eyes so deep that they looked like bruises.

He couldn't share the article with her. A year ago, she might have laughed. But now, tears would stream down her cheeks and she would want him to hold her. And when she woke up, he would hold her, because they had so little time left.

She didn't need to see the paragraph that stood out from the page as if someone had expanded the type:

...and with his loss, all of photography's pioneers are dead. In the United States alone we have lost, in recent

years, Alexander Gardiner, Samuel F. B. Morse, Edward and Henry Anthony, and Mathew B. Brady. Gardiner practiced the craft until his death, going west and sending some of the best images back home. The Anthonys sold many of their fine works in stereoscope for us all to see. Morse had other interests and quit photography to pursue them. Brady lost his eyesight after the War, and closed his studios here and in New York....

Perhaps he was wrong. Perhaps they wouldn't laugh together. Perhaps she would be as angry as he was. He hadn't died. He hadn't. No one allowed him to show his work any more. He hadn't even been to the gallery of his dreams since that confusing last dream, years ago.

Brady placed the newspaper with the others near the door. Then he crawled onto the bed and pulled Julia close. Her small body was comfort, and in her sleep, she turned and held him back.

1886

One morning, he whirled into a place of such emptiness it chilled his soul. The buildings were tall and white, the grass green, and the flowers in bloom. His wagon was the only black thing on the surface of this place. He could smell lilacs as he walked forward, and he thought of Julia resting at their apartment —too fragile now to even do her needlepoint.

This silence was worse than at the last place. Here it felt as if human beings had never touched this land, despite the buildings. He felt as if he were the only person alive.

He walked up the stone steps of the first building and pushed open the glass door. The room inside was empty— as empty as his gallery had been when he first dreamed it. No dust or footprints marred the white floor, no smudges covered the white walls. He looked out the window and, as he watched, a building twenty yards away shimmered and disappeared.

Brady shoved his hands in his pockets and scurried outside. Another, squarer building also disappeared. The shimmering was different, more ominous than the shimmering left by his benefactress. In these remains, he could almost see the debris, the dust from the buildings that had once been. He could feel the destruction and knew that these places weren't reappearing somewhere else. He ran to his wagon, climbed inside, and peered out at the world from the wagon's edge. And, as he watched, building after building winked out of existence.

He clutched the camera to him, but took no photographs. The smell of lilacs grew stronger. His hands were cold, shaking. He watched the buildings disappear until only a grassy field remained.

"You can't even photograph it."

Her appearance didn't surprise him. He expected her, after seeing the changes, perhaps because he had been thinking of her. Her hair was shoulder-length now, but other than that, she hadn't changed in all the years since he last saw her.

"It's so clean and neat," Her voice shook. "You can't even tell that anyone died here."

Brady crawled out of the wagon and stood beside her. He felt more uneasy here than he had felt under the shelling at the first battle of Bull Run. There at least he could hear the whistle, feel the explosions. Here the destruction came from nowhere.

"Welcome to war in my lifetime, Mathew." She crossed her arms in front of her chest. "Here we get rid of everything, not just a person's body, but all traces of their home, their livelihood—and, in most cases, any memories of them. I lost my son like this and I couldn't remember that he had existed until I started work on this project." She smiled just a little. "The time travel gives unexpected gifts, some we can program for, like improved eyesight or health, and some we can't, like improved memories. The scientists say it has something to do with molecular rearrangement, but that makes no sense to you, since most people didn't know what a molecule was in your day."

He stood beside her, his heart pounding in his throat. She turned to him, took his hand in hers.

"We can't go any farther than this, Mathew."

He frowned. "I'm done?"

"Yes. I can't thank you in the ways that I'd like. If I could, I'd send you back, give you money, let you rebuild your life from the war on. But I can't. We can't. But I can bring you to the exhibit when it opens, and hope that the response is what we expect. Would you like that, Mathew?"

He didn't know exactly what she meant, and he wasn't sure he cared. He wanted to keep making photographs, to keep working here with her. He had nothing else. "I could still help you. I'm sure there are a number of things to be done."

She shook her head, then kissed his forehead. "You need to go home to your Julia, and enjoy the time you have left. We'll see each other again, Mathew."

And then she started to whirl, to shimmer. Brady reached for her and his hand went through her into the heated air. This shimmer was different; it had a life to it. He felt a thin relief. She had traveled beyond him, but not out of existence. He leaned against the edge of his wagon and stared at the lilac bushes and the wind blowing through the grasses, trying to understand what she had just told him. He and the wagon sat alone, in a field where people had once built homes and lived quiet lives. Finally, at dusk, he too shimmered out of the blackness and back to his own quiet life.

1887

Only Levin and Brady stood beside the open grave. The wind ruffled Brady's hair, dried the tear tracks on his cheeks. He hadn't realized how small Julia's life had become. Most of the people at the funeral had been his friends, people who had come to console him.

He could hear the trees rustling behind him. The breeze carried a scent of lilacs—how appropriate, Julia dying in the spring so that her flower would bloom near her grave. She had been so beautiful when he met her, so popular. She had whittled her life down for him, because she had thought he needed her. And he had.

Levin took Brady's arm. "Come along, Uncle," Levin said.

Brady looked up at his nephew, the closest thing to a

child he and Julia had ever had. Levin's hair had started to recede, and he too wore thick glasses.

"I don't want to leave her," Brady said. "I've left her too much already."

"It's all right, Uncle," Levin said as he put his arm around Brady's waist and led him through the trees. "She understands."

Brady glanced back at the hole in the ground, at his wife's coffin, and at the two men who had already started to shovel dirt on top. "I know she understands," he said. "She always has."

1887

That night, Brady didn't sleep. He sat on the bed he had shared with Julia, and clutched her pillow against his chest. He missed her even breathing, her comfortable presence. He missed her hand on his cheek and her warm voice, reassuring him. He missed holding her, and loving her, and telling her how much he loved her.

It's all right, Uncle, Levin had said. *She understands.*

Brady got up, set the pillow down, and went to the window. She had looked out so many times, probably feeling alone, while he pursued his dreams of greatness.

She had never said what she thought these past few years, but he saw her look at him, saw the speculation in her eyes when he returned from one of his trips. She had loved him too much to question him.

Then he felt it: the odd sensation that always preceded

a whirling. But he was done—he hadn't left in over a year. He was just tired, just—

spinning. Colors and pain and dust bombarded him. Smells he would briefly catch and by the time he identified them they had disappeared. His head ached, his body felt as if it were being torn in fifteen different directions. And when he stopped, he stood in the gallery of his dreams... only he knew that he was wide awake.

It existed then. It really existed.

And it was full of people.

Women wore long clingy dresses in a shining material. Their hair varied in hue from brown to pink, and many had jewelry stapled into their noses, their cheeks and, in one case, along the rim of the eye. The men's clothes were as colorful and as shiny. They wore makeup, but no jewelry. A few people seemed out of place, in other clothes—a woman in combat fatigues from one of the wars Brady had seen, a man in dust-covered denim pants and a ripped shirt, another man dressed in all black leaning against a gallery door. All of the doors in the hallway were open and people spilled in and out, conversing or holding shocked hands to their throats.

The conversation was so thick that Brady couldn't hear separate voices, separate words. A variety of perfumes overwhelmed him and the coolness seemed to have left the gallery. He let the crowd push him down the hall toward

his own exhibit and as he passed, he caught bits and pieces
of other signs:

...IMAGE ARTIST...

...(2000-2010)...

...HOLOGRAPHER, AFRICAN BIOLOGICAL...

...ABC CAMERAMAN, LEBANON...

....PHOTOJOURNALIST, VIETNAM CONFLICT...

...(1963)...

...NEWS REELS FROM THE PACIFIC THEATER...

...OFFICIAL PHOTOGRAPHER, WORLD WAR I...

...(1892-...

...INDIAN WARS...

And then his own:

MATHEW B. BRADY EXHIBIT

OFFICIAL PHOTOGRAPHER:

UNITED STATES CIVIL WAR

(1861-1865)

The room was full. People stood along the walls, gazing
at his portraits, discussing and pointing at the fields of
honored dead. One woman turned away from the toddler,
shot in the back; another from the burning church. People
looked inside Brady's wagon, and more than a few stared

at the portraits of him, lined along the Doric columns like a series of somber, aging men.

He caught a few words:

"Fantastic composition"..."amazing things with black and white"..."almost looks real"..."turns my stomach"... "can't imagine working with such primitive equipment"....

Someone touched his shoulder. Brady turned. A woman smiled at him. She wore a long purple gown and her brown hair was wrapped around the top of her head. It took a moment for him to recognize his benefactress.

"Welcome to the exhibit, Mathew. People are enjoying your work."

She smiled at him and moved on. And then it hit him. He finally had an exhibit. He finally had people staring at his work, and seeing what had really happened in all those places during all that time. She had shown him this gallery all his life, whirled him here when he thought he was asleep. This was his destiny, just as dying impoverished in his own world was his destiny.

"You're the artist?" A slim man in a dark suit stood beside Brady.

"This is my work," Brady said.

A few people crowded around. The scent of soap and perfume nearly overwhelmed him.

"I think you're an absolutely amazing talent," the man said. His voice was thin, with an accent that seemed British but wasn't. "I can't believe the kind of work you put into this to create such stark beauty. And with such bulky equipment."

"Beauty?" Brady could barely let the word out of his throat. He gazed around the room, saw the flowered woman, the row of corpses on the Gettysburg Battlefield.

"Eerie," a woman said. "Rather like late Goya, don't you think, Lavinia?"

Another woman nodded. "Stunning, the way you captured the exact right light, the exact moment to illuminate the concept."

"Concept?" Brady felt his hands shake. "You're looking at war here. People died in these portraits. This is history, not art."

"I think you're underestimating your work," the man said. "It is truly art, and you are a great, great artist. Only an artist would see how to use black and white to such a devastating effect—"

"I wasn't creating art," Brady said. "My assistants and I, we were shot at. I nearly died the day the soldiers burned that church. This isn't beauty. This is war. It's truth. I wanted you to see how ugly war really is."

"And you did it so well," the man said. "I truly admire your technique." And then he walked out of the room. Brady watched him go. The women smiled, shook his hand, told him that it was a pleasure to meet him. He wandered around the room, heard the same types of conversation, and stopped when he saw his benefactress.

"They don't understand," he said. "They think this was done for them, for their appreciation. They're calling this art."

"It is art, Mathew," she said softly. She glanced around the room, as if she wanted to be elsewhere.

"No, he said. "It actually happened."

"A long time ago." She patted his hand. "The message about war and destruction will go home in their subconscious. They will remember this." And then she turned her back on him and pushed her way through the crowd. Brady tried to follow her, but only made it as far as his wagon. He sat on its edge and buried his face in his hands.

He sat there for a long time, letting the conversation hum around him, wondering at his own folly. And then he heard his name called in a voice that made his heart rise.

"Mr. Brady?"

He looked up and saw Julia. Not the Julia who had grown pale and thin in their small apartment, but the Julia he had met so many years ago. She was slender and young, her face glowing with health. No gray marked her ringlets, and her hoops were wide with a fashion decades old. He reached out his hands. "Julia."

She took his hands and sat beside him on the wagon, her young-girl face turned in a smile. "They think you're wonderful, Mr. Brady."

"They don't understand what I've done. They think it's art—" he stopped himself. This wasn't his Julia. This was the young girl, the one who had danced with him, who had told him about her dream. She had come from a different place and a different time, the only time she had seen the effects of his work.

He looked at her then, really looked at her, saw the shine in her blue eyes, the blush to her cheeks. She was watching the people look at his portraits, soaking in the discussion. Her gloved hand clutched his, and he could feel her wonderment and joy.

"I would be so proud if this were my doing. Mr. Brady. Imagine a room like this filled with your vision, your work."

He didn't look at the room. He looked at her. This moment, this was what kept her going all those years. The memory of what she thought was a dream, of what she hoped would become real. And it was real, but not in any way she understood. Perhaps, then, he didn't understand it either.

She turned to him, smiled into his face. "I would so like to be a part of this," she said. She thought it was a dream; otherwise she would have never spoken so boldly. No, wait. She had been bold when she was young.

"You will be," Brady said. And until that moment, he never realized how much a part of it she had been, always standing beside him, always believing in him even when he no longer believed in himself. She had made the greater sacrifice—her entire life for his dream, his vision, his work.

"Julia," he said, thankful for this last chance to touch her, this last chance to hold her. "I could not do this without you. You made it all possible."

She leaned against him and laughed, a fluted sound he hadn't heard in decades. "But it's your work that they admire, Mr. Brady. Your work."

"They call me an artist."

"That's right." Her words were crisp, sure. "An artist's work lives beyond him. This isn't our world, Mr. Brady. In the other rooms, the pictures move."

The pictures move. He had been given a gift, to see his own future. To know that the losses he suffered, the reversals he and Julia had lived through weren't all for nothing. How many people got even that?

He tucked her arm in his. He had to be out of this room, out of this exhibit he didn't really understand. They stood together, her hoop clearing a path for them in the crowd. He stopped and surveyed the four walls—filled with his portraits, portraits of places most of these people had never seen—his memories that they shared and made their own.

Then he stepped out of the exhibit into a future in which he would never take part, perhaps to gain a perspective he had never had before.

And all the while, Julia remained beside him.

YOU MIGHT LIKE THIS...

THE END OF THE WORLD

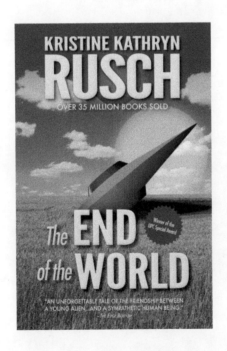

THEN

The air reeked of smoke.

The people ran, and the others chased them.

She kept tripping. Momma pulled her forward, but Momma's hand was slippery. Her hand slid out, and she fell, sprawling on the wooden sidewalk.

Momma reached for her, but the crowd swept Momma forward.

All she saw was Momma's face, panicked, her hands, grasping, and then Momma was gone.

Everyone ran around her, over her, on her. She put her hands over her head and cringed, curling herself into a little ball.

She made herself change color. Brown-gray like the sidewalk, with black lines running up and down.

Dress hems skimmed over her. Boots brushed her. Heels pinched the skin on her arms.

No spikes, Momma always said. *No spikes or they'll know.*

So she held her breath, hoping the spikes wouldn't break through her skin because she was so scared, and her side hurt where someone's boot hit it, and the wooden sidewalk bounced as more and more people ran past her.

Finally, she started squinching, like Daddy taught her before he left.

Slide, he said. *A little bit at a time. Slide. Squinch onto whatever surface you're on and cling.*

It was hard to squinch without spikes, but she did, her head tucked in her belly, her hair trailing to one side. More boots stomped on it, pulling it, but she bit her lower lip so that she wouldn't have to think about the pain.

She was almost to the bank door when the sidewalk stopped shaking. No one ran by her. She was alone.

She flattened herself against the brick and shuddered. Her skin smelled of chewing tobacco, spit and beer from the saloon next door.

She had shut down her ears, but she finally rotated them outward. Men were shouting, women yelling. There was pounding and screaming and a high-pitched noise she didn't like.

If they found her flattened against the brick, they'd know. If they saw the spikes rise from her body, they'd know. If they saw her squinching, they'd know.

But she couldn't move.

She was shivering, and she didn't know what to do.

NOW

The call didn't come through channels. It rang to Becca Keller's personal cell.

Chase Waterston hadn't even said hello.

"Got a problem at the End of the World," he'd said, his usually self-assured voice shaky. "Can you get here right away? Just you."

Normally, she would have told him to call the precinct or 911, but something stopped her. Probably that scared edge to his voice, a sound she'd never heard in all the years she'd known him.

She drove from the center of downtown Hope to the End of the World, a drive that, in the old days, would have taken five minutes. Now it took twenty, and the only thing that kept her from being annoyed at the traffic were the mountains, bleak and cold, rising up like goddesses at the edge of Hope.

Hope was a mountain city, but its terrain was high desert. Vast expanses of brown still marked the outskirts of town, although the interior had lost much of its desert feel. By the time she passed the latest ticky-tacky development, she hit the rolling dunes of her childhood. Even though she had on the air-conditioning, the smell of sagebrush blew in —full of promise.

If she kept going straight too much farther, she'd hit small windy roads filled with switchbacks that led to now-trendy ski resorts. If she turned right, she'd follow the old stage coach route over the edge of the mountains into the Willamette Valley where most of Oregon's population lived.

The End of the World was an ancient resort at the fork between the mountain roads and the old stagecoach route. At the turn of the previous century, some enterprising entrepreneur figured travelers who were taking the narrow road toward the Willamette Valley would welcome a place to rest and recover from the long dusty trip.

Now bumper-to-bumper traffic filled that wagon route, which had expanded to a four-lane highway. Hope actually had a real rush hour, thanks to ex-patriate Californians, retired baby boomers, and ridiculously cheap housing.

Chase was rebuilding the resort for those baby boomers and Californians. For some reason, he thought they'd want to stay in a hundred-year-old hotel, with a view of the mountains and the river, even in the heat of the summer and the deep cold of the desert winter.

Becca steered the squad with her left hand and fiddled with the air-conditioner with her right, wishing her own car was out of the shop. No matter what she did, she couldn't get the squad car cooled. Nothing seemed to be working properly. Or maybe that was the effect of the heat.

It was a hundred and three degrees, and the third week without rain. The radio's most recent weather report promised the temperature would reach one hundred and eight by the time the day was over.

Finally, she reached the construction site.

Chase had set up the site so that it only blocked part of the ever-present wind and as a consequence, the dust billowed across the highway with the gusts.

The city had cited Chase twice for the hazard, and he'd promised to fix it just after the Fourth of July holiday. It looked like he'd been keeping his word, too. A huge plastic construction fence leaned against the old building. Graders and post-diggers were parked on the side of the road.

Nothing moved. Not the cats Chase had been using to dig out the old parking lot, not the crane he'd rented the week before, and not the crew, most of whom sat on the backs of pick-up trucks, their faces blackened with dust and grime and too much sun. She could see their eyes, white against the darkness of their skins, watching her as she turned onto the dirt path that Chase had been using as an access road.

He was waiting for her in the doorway of what had once been a natatorium. Built over an old underground spring, the Natatorium had once boasted the largest swimming pool in Eastern Oregon. There was some kind of pipe system which pumped water into the pool, keeping it perpetually cold. In the Natatorium's heyday, the water had been replaced daily.

Behind the Natatorium was the old five-story brick hotel that still had the original fixtures. No vandals had ever attacked the place. Even the windows were intact.

Becca had gone inside more than once, first as an impressionable twelve-year-old, and ever since, part of her believed the rumors that the hotel was haunted.

She pulled up beside the Natatorium door, in a tiny patch of shade provided by the overhanging roof. She got out and the blast-furnace heat hit her, prickling sweat on her skin almost instantly. Apparently the air conditioner had been working in the piece-of-crap squad after all.

Chase watched her. His lips were chapped, his skin fried blackish red from the sun. He had weather-wrinkles around his eyes and narrow mouth. His hair was cropped short, and over it he wore a regulation hardhat. He clutched another one in his left hand, slapping it rhythmically against his thigh.

"Thanks for coming, Becca," he said, and he still sounded shaken.

The tone was unfamiliar, but the expression on his face wasn't. She'd seen it only once, after she'd told him she wanted out, that his values and hers were so different, she couldn't stomach a relationship any longer.

"What do you got, Chase?" she asked.

"Come with me." He handed her the hardhat he'd been holding.

She took it as a gust of wind caught her short hair and blew its clipped edges into her face. She slipped the hardhat on, and tucked her hair underneath it, then followed Chase inside the building.

It was hotter inside the Natatorium, and the air smelled of rot and mold. She usually thought of those as humidity smells, but the Natatorium's interior was so dry that it was crumbly.

The floor was shredded with age, the wood so brittle that she wondered if it would hold her weight. Most of the walls were gone, the remains of them piled in a corner. Chase had gutted the interior.

When she had been a girl, she had played in this place. Her parents had forbidden her to come, which made it all the more inviting. The rot and mold smells had been present even then. But the walls had still been up, and there had been some ancient furniture in here as well, made unusable by weather and critters chewing the interior.

She used to stand inside the entrance with the door open, the stream of sunlight carrying a spinning tunnel of dust motes. When she closed her eyes halfway, she could just imagine the people arriving here after a long day of travel, happy to be in a place of such elegance, such warmth.

But now even that sense of a long ago but lively past was gone, and all that remained was the shell of the building itself—a hazard, an eyesore, something to be torn down and replaced.

Chase's boots echoed on the wood floor. He led her along the edges, pointing at holes closer to the center. She wondered if any of his employees had caused the holes, walking imprudently across the floor, foot catching on the weak spot, and then slipping through.

He was taking her to the employees' staircase in the back. When they reached it, she saw why. It was made of metal. Rusted metal, but metal all the same. Someone had recently bolted the stairs into the wall, probably under Chase's orders. A metal hand railing had been reinforced as well.

Chase looked over his shoulder to make sure she was following. She caught a glimpse of something in his face— reluctance? Fear? She couldn't quite tell—and then, as suddenly as it appeared, it was gone.

He went down the steps two at a time. She followed. Even though the handrail had been rebolted, the metal still flaked under her hand. The bolts might hold if she suddenly fell through the stairs but she wasn't sure if the railing would.

The smell grew stronger here, as if the mold had somehow managed to survive the dry summers. The farther down she went, the cooler the air got. It was still hot, but no longer oppressive.

Chase stopped at the bottom of the stairs. He watched her come down the last few, his gaze holding hers. The intensity of his gaze startled her. It was vulnerable, in a way she hadn't seen since their first year together.

Then he stepped away so that she could stand on the floor below.

The smell was so strong that it overwhelmed her. Beneath the mold and rot, there was something else, something familiar, something foul. It made the hair rise on the back of her neck.

"That way," Chase said, and this time she wasn't mistaking it. His voice was shaking. "I'll wait here."

She frowned at him, and then kept going. The floor here was covered in ceramic tile, chipped and broken, but sturdy. She wondered what was beneath it. Ground? Old-fashioned concrete? Wood? She couldn't tell. But the floor didn't creak here, and it felt solid.

A long wall hid everything from view. A door stood

open, sending in sunlight filled with dust motes, just like she remembered. Only there shouldn't be sunlight here. This was the basement, the miraculous swimming pool, the place that had helped make the End of the World famous.

She stepped through the door.

The light came from the back wall—or what had been the back. Chase's crew had destroyed this part of the building.

The basement of the End of the World was open to the air for the first time since it had been completed.

That strange feeling she'd had since she reached the bottom of the stairs grew. If the basement wasn't sealed, then the stench shouldn't have been so strong. The old air should have escaped, letting the freshness of the desert inside.

Some of the heat had trickled in, but not enough to dissipate the natural coolness. She stepped forward. The tile on the other side of the pool was hidden under mounds of dirt. The pool itself was half destroyed, but the cat which had done the damage wasn't anywhere near it. She could see the big tire tracks, scored deeply into the sandy earth, as if the cat itself had been stuck or if the operator had tried to escape in a hurry.

They had uncovered something. That much was clear. And she was beginning to get an idea as to what it was.

A body.

Given the smell, it had to have died here recently. Bodies didn't decay in the desert—not in the dry air and the sand. Inside a building like this, there might be standard decomposition, but considering how hot it had been, even that seemed unlikely.

She'd have to assume cause of death was suspicious because the body had been located here. And then she'd have to figure out a way to find out whose body it was.

She was already planning how she'd conduct her case when she stepped off the tile onto a mound of dirt, and peered into the gaping hole, and saw—

Bones. Piles of bones. Recognizable bones. Femurs, hip bones, pelvic bones, rib cages. Hundreds of human bones. And more skulls than she could count.

She rocked back on her heels, pressing her free hand to her face, the smell—the illogical and impossible smell—now turning her stomach.

A mass grave, of the kind she'd only seen in film or police academy photos.

A mass grave, anywhere from a hundred to seventy-five years old.

A mass grave, in Hope. She hadn't even heard rumors of it, and she had lived here all her life.

"Son of a bitch," she said.

"Yeah," Chase said from the stairs, "I couldn't agree more."

THEN

The screaming sent ripples through her. She couldn't complete the change. She couldn't even assume the color and texture of the brick.

Tears pricked her eyes. Tears, as big a giveaway as her hair, her fingers, her ears. Somehow, when she stopped the spikes, she stopped all her abilities.

Or maybe it was just the fear.

A door squeaked open, then boots hit the sidewalk. Polished boots with only a layer of black dust along the edge. Men's boots, not the dainty things Momma tried to wear.

She tried to will the shivering away, but she couldn't.

She couldn't move at all.

Not that she had anywhere to go.

She could only pray that he wouldn't look down, that he wouldn't see her, that she would be safe for just a little longer.

NOW

Becca stared at the hole. She couldn't even count all the skulls, rising like white stones out of the dirt. Not to mention the rib cages off to one side or the tiny bones lying in a corner, bones that probably belonged in a hand or a foot.

She couldn't do much on her own. But she could find out where that stink was coming from.

She turned around and headed for the stairs.

Chase tipped his hardhat back, revealing his dark eyes. "Where're you going?"

"To get some things from my evidence bag," Becca said.

"You're not going to call anyone, are you?" he asked.

She stopped in front of him. "I can't take care of this alone. You should know that."

He leaned against the railing, that assumed casual gesture which meant he was the most distressed. "This'll ruin me, Becca. Half my capital is in this place."

"You told me no good businessman ever invests his own money," she snapped, mostly because she was surprised.

He shrugged. "Guess I'm not a good businessman."

But he was. He had restored three of the downtown's oldest buildings, making them into expensive condominiums with views of the mountains. Single-handedly, he'd revitalized Hope's downtown, by adding trendy stores that the locals claimed would never succeed (yet somehow they did, thanks to the "foreigners," as the Californians were called) and restaurants so upscale that Becca would have to spend half a week's pay just to eat lunch.

"You knew I'd go by the book when you called me here," she said, more sharply than she intended. He'd gotten to her. That was the problem; he always did.

"I thought maybe we could talk. They're old bones. If we can get someone to recover them and keep it quiet—"

"How many workers saw this?" she asked. "Do you think they'll keep it quiet?"

"If I pay them enough," he said. "And if we move the bones to a proper cemetery."

"Is that what you think this is?" she asked. "A graveyard?"

"Isn't it?" He seemed genuinely surprised. "It was so far out in the desert when this place was built that it's possible —no, it's probable—that the memory of the graveyard got lost."

"I saw at least two ribcages with shattered bones, and several skulls looked crushed."

His lips trembled, and it was a moment before he spoke. "The equipment could have done that."

But he didn't sound convinced.

"It could have," she said. "But we need to know."

"Why?" he asked.

She looked over her shoulder. That patch of sunlight still glinted through the hole in the wall. The dust motes still floated. If she didn't look down, the place would seem just as beautiful and interesting as it always had.

"Because someone loved them once. Someone probably wants to know what happened to them."

"Someone?" He snorted. "Becca, the pool was put over a tennis court that was built at the turn of the 20th century. No one remembers these people. Only historians would care."

He paused, and she felt her breath catch.

Then he said, "This is my life."

He used a tone and inflection she used to find particularly mesmerizing. Once she told their couples therapist that with that tone, he could convince her to do anything, and that was when the therapist told her that she had to get out.

"It's a crime scene," Becca said, knowing that the argument was weak.

"You don't know that for sure, and even if it is, it's a hundred years old," he said.

"Then what's the smell?"

He frowned, clearly not understanding her.

"This is a desert, Chase. Bodies buried in dirt in a dry climate don't decay. They mummify."

He blinked. He obviously hadn't thought of that.

"And," she said, "even if they had decayed because of some strange environmental reason particular to this basement, they wouldn't smell after a hundred years."

That guarded expression had returned to his face. Only his eyes moved now.

"Maybe it's something small," he said. "A mouse, someone's lost cat."

She shook her head. "Smell's too strong, and over the entire building. If it were something small, the smell would have faded back when you broke open that wall."

"Not when it was dug up?" he asked, seeming surprised.

"No," she said. "Is that when you first smelled it?"

"That's when they called me."

They, meaning his crew. She frowned at him, wondering if he was going to blame them.

But for what? A smell?

She'd have to find the source before she made assumptions.

And that, she knew, was going to be hard.

THEN

A hand touched her shoulder. A human hand, warm and gentle. Another shivery ripple ran through her. She still had a shoulder; she hadn't gotten rid of that either. How silly she must look, plastered against the brick wall like a half formed younglin.

Screams still echoed. The shouts had died down, although sometimes they rose up altogether, like a group got excited about something.

"You're one of them, aren't you?"

Male voice, human, just as gentle as the hand. She couldn't stop shivering.

"I won't hurt you."

She resisted the urge to rotate an eye upwards, so that she could see more than the boot.

"But you better come with me before they find you."

That did startle her. Her eye moved before she could stop it. It formed above her shoulder. He jumped back slightly when her eye appeared, but his hand never left her skin, even though it was finally turning tannish-red like the brick.

She'd seen him before. Daddy had laughed with him in the good days. He had slicked-back hair and a narrow face and kind eyes.

He crouched beside her, and looked right at her eye, like it didn't bother him, even though she knew it did. He wouldn't've jumped like that if it didn't.

"Please," he said, "come with me. I don't know when they're coming back. And someone might see us. Please."

She had to form a mouth. Her nose remained, tucked against her stomach from when she'd formed a ball, but her mouth had disappeared when she had tried to take on the appearance of the wooden sidewalk.

It took all her strength to make the mouth come out near the eye, and from the look of disgust that passed over his face, she still didn't look right. Her hair was on the other side of her body, and her eye was just above her shoulder. The mouth had probably come out on what would have been her back if she put herself together right.

Right being human.

That's what Momma said.

Momma.

"Please," he said again, and this time, she heard panic in his voice.

"Stuck," she said.

"Oh, Christ." He looked up and down the street, then at the buildings across from it.

He seemed younger than she remembered, or maybe she was as bad at telling human ages as Momma was.

"How do we get you unstuck?" he asked.

She didn't know. She'd never been like this, not this scared, not all by herself.

She tried to shrug and felt her other shoulder form into the wood. A splinter dug into her skin, and her entire body turned red with pain.

"What a mess," he said, and she didn't know if he meant her or what was going on or how scared they both seemed to be.

She willed herself to let go, but she was attached to the brick, and she'd lost control of half her body functions. Daddy said fear would do that.

Whatever happens, baby, he'd say, *you have to trust us. You have to believe we'll get together again. Let that be your strength, so that you never, ever succumb to fear.*

But he'd been gone for a long time now. And Momma hadn't come back for her, even though people were screaming.

The man tried to pry a flat corner of her skin from the edge of the brick. She could feel the tug, saw his face scrunch up in disgust when he got to the sticky underneath part.

"How'd you get there?" he asked.

"Squinched," she said.

"Squinched." He didn't understand. And she spoke his language, she knew she did. She formed the right mouth, she'd been using the words for a long time now, and she knew how they felt inside her brain and out.

"Can you show me?" he asked. "Can you squinch onto my arm?"

She wasn't supposed to squinch to a human. Momma was strict about that. Like there was something bad about it, something awful would happen.

But something awful was happening now.

The screams...

"No," she said, even though that had to be a lie. Momma and Daddy wouldn't forbid something if she couldn't've done it in the first place.

"God," he said, then looked down the street where the screams had come from. Where the shouts had grown more and more angry every time they rose up.

Right now, it was quiet, and she hated that more.

She hated it all.

"Stay here," he said.

He stood up, letting go of her shoulder. The warm vanished, and the fear rose even worse. Her other shoulder disappeared, and she felt the spikes, threatening to appear.

She had to close both eyes and will the spikes away.

When she opened the eyes, he was gone.

She moved the eyes all over her skin, looking for him, and she didn't see him at all.

The street was still empty, and too quiet.

Then, faraway, someone laughed. A mean, nasty, brittle laugh.

She folded her ears inside her skin, and willed herself flat, hoping, this time, that it would work.

NOW

Becca climbed the stairs, clinging to the handrail, the rust flaking against her palms. She had to call for help. At most, she needed a coroner, and probably a few officers just to search for the source of that smell.

But she felt guilty about calling. Chase used to talk about restoring the End of the World when she'd met him. He had brought her out here on their first date, even though she'd told him that she had explored the property repeatedly when she was a child.

Maybe they'd be able to keep this out of the paper, particularly if it turned out to be a graveyard or a dumping ground. But even that probably wouldn't happen.

The newspapers seemed to love this kind of story.

If she reported this, she would condemn Chase's

project to a kind of limbo. With so much capital invested, he probably couldn't afford to wait until the legal issues were solved.

She almost turned around to ask him how much time he could give them, but then she'd be compromising the investigation. For all she knew, there was a recently killed human beneath that dirt, and someone (Chase?) was using the old bones to hide it.

Then she shook her head. Not Chase. He was manipulative and difficult, moody and untrustworthy, but he wasn't—nor had he ever been—violent.

She sighed and continued up the stairs. Much as she wanted to help him, she couldn't. She had an obligation to the entire community.

She had an obligation to herself.

The wind hit her the moment she stepped outside. Bits of sand stung her skin, sticking to the sweat. Even with the sun, it now felt cooler out here because of that wind.

The construction workers watched her. She didn't know most of them; the town had grown too big for her to know everyone by sight like she had when she was a child. Many of these workers were Hispanic, some of them probably illegal.

Hispanics expected her to check their papers. She was supposed to do that too, although she never did. She didn't object to people who worked hard and tried to improve their lives.

With one hand, she tipped her hardhat back and nodded toward the workers. Then she opened the squad's driver's door, and winced at the heat which poured out at her. She leaned inside, unwilling to go into that heat voluntarily, and grabbed the radio's handset.

She paused before turning it on, knowing that even that momentary hesitation was a victory for Chase.

Then she clicked the handset and asked the dispatch to send Jillian Mills.

Jillian Mills was the head coroner for Hope and the surrounding counties. She actually worked the job full time, but her assistants were dentists and veterinarians, and one retired doctor.

"You want the crime scene unit?" the dispatch asked. It was standard procedure for a crime scene unit to come with the coroner.

"Not yet," Becca said. "I'm not sure what exactly we have here, except that it's dead."

Which was technically true, if she ignored all the crushed and broken bones.

"Tell her to hurry," Becca added. "It's hot as hell out here and there's a construction crew waiting."

That usually worked to get any city official moving. Lately, the "foreigners" had taken to suing the city if their emergency or official personnel delayed money-making operations, even for a day.

Chase would never do that—he knew that getting

along with the city helped his permits go through and his iffy projects get approved—but Becca still used the excuse.

She didn't want to be here any longer than she had to.

She stood, lifted her hardhat, and wiped the sweat off her forehead. Then she closed the door and leaned on it for a moment.

The End of the World.

She wondered if Chase had ever thought that the name might have been prophetic.

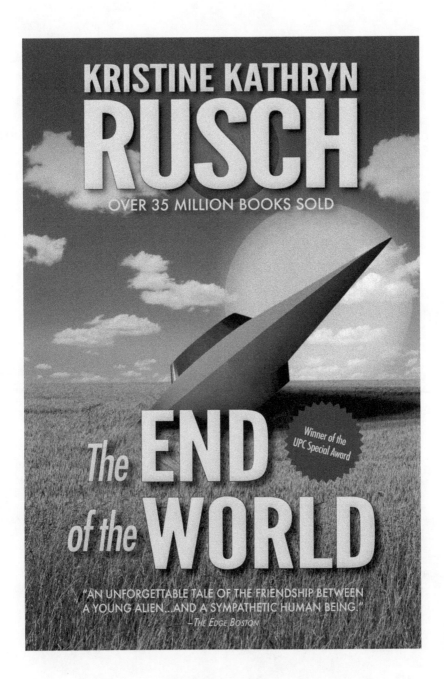

Keep Reading *The End of the World!*

Go to www.wmgbooks.com

HEAR DIRECTLY FROM KRIS

Sign up for the Kristine Kathryn Rusch newsletter and hear directly from Kris herself.

Go to kriswrites.com.

Get the latest news and releases from all of the WMG authors and lines, including Kristine Kathryn Rusch, Kristine Grayson, Kris Nelscott, Dean Wesley Smith, *Pulphouse Fiction Magazine, Smith's Monthly,* and so much more.

Go to wmgbooks.com.

You can also follow Kris on Bookbub.

We value honest feedback, and would love to hear your opinion in a review, if you're so inclined, on your favorite book retailer's site.

ABOUT THE AUTHOR

New York Times bestselling author Kristine Kathryn Rusch writes in almost every genre. Her novels have made bestseller lists around the world and her short fiction has appeared in eighteen best of the year collections. She has won more than twenty-five awards for her fiction, including the Hugo, Le Prix Imaginales, the Asimov's Readers Choice award, and the Ellery Queen Mystery Magazine Readers Choice Award.

Rusch writes in many genres, from science fiction to mystery, from western to romance. She has written under a pile of pen names, but most of her work appears as Kristine Kathryn Rusch. Her Kris Nelscott pen name has won or been nominated for most of the awards in the mystery genre, and her Kristine Grayson pen name became a bestseller in romance. Her science fiction novels set in the bestselling Diving Universe have won dozens of awards and are in development for a major TV show. She also writes the Retrieval Artist sf series and several major series that mostly appear as short fiction.

Rusch broke a number of barriers in the sf/f field, including being the first female editor of *The Magazine of Fantasy & Science Fiction*. She has owned two different publishing companies, and writes a highly regarded publishing industry blog on Patreon. She also writes a highly regarded weekly publishing industry blog. Find out more about her work at kriswrites.com, and more on all her books at wmgbooks.com.

facebook.com/kristinekathrynruschwriter
patreon.com/kristinekathrynrusch
bookbub.com/authors/kristine-kathryn-rusch